THE MANGROVES

A Novella

John L. Campbell

Stephanie,

This story might stay in your head for a while...

This is a work of fiction. Names, characters, places and incidents either are products of the author's imagination or are used fictitiously. Any resemblance to actual events or locales or persons, living or dead, is entirely coincidental.

Visit the author at www.johnlcampbell.com

Cover design and illustration by Keith Haney /
Haney@xmission.com

Printed in the United States of America

In Memory of
CECIL L. CAMPBELL
1935 – 2009

The best man I've ever known.

THE MANGROVES

1

The sea spoke to him in a voice of wind and gulls. A sparkling, pale blue, it pushed against the beach below with a hiss, then slipped away. Fresh and salty, its breeze rustled the palm leaves and bent the sea grass before it, cooling the young man's skin. It was a clean thing, this sea. Capable of cleansing a soul. And so very far from his home.

Shoji stood at the top of the dune and took it in, breathing deeply. A brown pelican stood on the sand not far away, the wind ruffling its feathers as it too looked out to sea. A moment later it lifted off, ungainly and large, carving at the air with its big wings until it had altitude and was sailing out over the waves. Shoji closed his eyes, the sun warm upon his face, and for just a moment he was that pelican, turning slowly over the sea, floating on the updraft, weightless and free. He spread his arms slowly, the breeze whipping his sleeves, and he imagined it carrying him up, up, far from this place, out over that crystalline water, high into the clouds and oblivion.

The whine of an incoming round broke the moment, and he turned, jumping down into the trench and ducking into the log-covered shelter. More streaked in, the booming of the fifteen-inch naval guns echoing over the water. Explosions now as they landed, some close on the beach, others behind the bunker, inside the perimeter. The earth shook with their impact, dirt and stones rattling across the overhead cover. Still more howled in, the guns working into a steady rhythm.

Shoji sat on an ammo crate and sipped from a canteen, then began polishing the lenses of his wire-rimmed glasses while he looked around at the boys in the bunker with him. There were six of them, all from 2nd squad, and not one over nineteen. They jumped and cast fearful glances at the logs above with every impact, gripping their weapons tightly. A couple mouthed soft prayers, and one was weeping silently, his arms wrapped around his head. No one comforted him.

"How long before they stop?" shouted Matsuda, a seventeen-year-old only recently arrived, one of the last replacements to land before the enemy sealed off the island a few weeks ago. He was a fisherman who had been plucked from his family by an army desperate for bodies, rushed through a basic rifleman's course and then hurled into the maelstrom. Shoji saw that the boy was yelling at him.

"They've only just started," he replied. "This isn't your first shelling."

Matsuda shook his head. "Never like this!"

Shoji smiled. Every shelling was the worst anyone could imagine, far worse than any before.

A round landed close enough to lift the log roof several inches and blast hot air into the bunker. The explosion drowned out the unison of screams. Dust rolled in through the opening, and Shoji tied a white handkerchief across his face, tucking away his glasses.

Shorter, hollow-sounding booms joined the bigger guns, lofting 5.25-inch rounds onto the shore. That would be the light cruiser, Shoji knew, joining the much larger battleship. They had both been loitering insolently offshore for weeks, dashing in close when they chose to hammer the island, then steaming back out, fearless and untouchable. And why shouldn't they be? The British marines had captured the airfield weeks ago, and there hadn't been a Japanese plane in these skies for weeks before that. They had nothing to fear. The only thing which could stop them now was running out of shells, and of course their supply ships would rearm them before that ever happened.

The ground trembled with the shocks, and when one of the rounds blew sections of beach into the sky, the air was filled with a hissing sound as the sand fell back to earth. Most of the projectiles sailed overhead and past. Shoji tried not to think about it. It wasn't that he didn't feel afraid, and even now the thought of being torn apart in a fiery blast made him uncomfortable, but the bombardments didn't terrify him the way they used to.

Little about war did, anymore. As for the barrage, it would end when it ended, and there was nothing to be done about it but sit and wait. If one of the enemy's guns dropped a round on top of the bunker, then for him and his men, the barrage would just end that much sooner. His regret of the moment was the close, dirt-filled air and heat within the bunker, the dust making it difficult to see. He closed his eyes and imagined himself back atop the dune, breathing in the sea.

A figure leaped into the trench beyond the opening and rushed inside. One of the boys cried out and scrambled to lift his rifle, but Shoji stood and slapped it aside, towering over the young soldier. "Do you think a British marine would just run into our bunker? He would clear it first with a grenade." He smacked the boy lightly on the helmet. "You know better."

The boy looked at his boots in embarrassment, and Shoji turned to face the newcomer. Another boy in khaki, a regimental runner. The boy saluted. "Lieutenant Kichida, you are ordered to regimental headquarters at once."

Shoji nodded, then snapped on his pistol belt and hung his sword from it. He tucked his soft cap inside his tunic and put on a helmet. "Corporal Aoki," he said without looking at his radioman, "are you ready?"

The corporal had already shrugged into his bulky pack radio and slung his rifle. "Yes, sir."

The runner turned and held onto the log frame of the entry, took several deep breaths, then sprinted outside and scrambled up the trench wall. Shoji and his radioman followed. Once they were above the trench, they ran hunched over, more out of instinct than for any real added safety. An exploding shell would cut them in half regardless, upright or crouched. The fifty men of Shoji's platoon were spread out along the western perimeter, broken into half-squads and hidden within bunkers on the inland side of the dunes, all linked by interconnecting trenches. The young lieutenant glanced in both directions, able to pick out some of the flat log overheads, and was relieved to see all were intact. The landscape around him was another story.

Fountains of dark earth erupted into the sky around the three running men, the blasts deafening, clods of dirt peppering the ground and fine curtains of sand hanging in the air. The terrain, once covered in soft sea grass, had been transformed over the past weeks into tortured fields of craters, the soil resembling fields freshly plowed and ready for planting. Collapsed trenches and shattered bunkers could be seen in places, their splintered logs poking at odd angles out of the earth. A twisted howitzer jutted from a crater along with the bones and rotting flesh of its former crew, and the cab of a truck could be seen peering out of another, the rest of it hammered flat by a direct hit. Another truck was burning in the distance to the left, its flaming tires adding black smoke which hugged the ground.

In theory, they should have been able to stay within the trench network to reach the headquarters bunker without exposing themselves to flying shrapnel, but that was a fantasy. Even if the trenches weren't already collapsed or choked with debris and fallen palm trees, it would take triple the time to wind their way across the encampment, and that meant three times the chance of being hit. Straight across was quicker. The men did, however, take advantage of every trench or crater they came upon, jumping in and crouching for a moment to catch their breath or ride out a particularly heavy series of incoming rounds before clambering back out again to start running again. Shoji ran last, letting Cpl. Aoki follow the runner, intent upon making sure his radioman didn't fall behind with his heavy burden.

A shell from one of the battleship's bigger cannons streaked down and made a direct hit on a bunker fifty yards to their left. The blast threw the men flat as shrapnel and splinters of wood slashed overhead. Through his ringing ears Shoji thought he heard screaming, but he shook his head as he climbed once more to his feet. Impossible. No one could have lived through that. He was just glad it wasn't one of his bunkers, and worried about being away from his boys. Not that his presence would do anything to keep them alive should a round find their hiding place, but he worried nonetheless.

The runner darted around a twisted pile of blackened steel which had once been an anti-aircraft gun, then disappeared into a trench, followed by Aoki. When Shoji jumped down a moment later, he was disoriented, looking in both directions but not seeing the two men, and unsure if the headquarters was to the left or right. He crouched as more explosions ripped the earth above, wincing and squinting into the dust. Then he saw a darker spot along the far wall of the trench to his right, an opening with a flap of canvas covering it. He headed for it and ducked inside a small, concrete-walled ante-chamber, running into Cpl. Aoki's radio pack. The man grunted and struggled to move to the side in the cramped space to allow his officer to get past.

The regimental headquarters bunker was a series of low-ceilinged rooms reinforced by concrete and buried under earth, logs and layers of sheet steel. Lanterns glowed from where they hung on the walls, and shapes moved through the gloom. Shoji replaced his helmet with his soft cap, put on his glasses and took a moment to let his eyes adjust, then began shouldering his way through the men in the tight space. He had been here many times, and knew where to go. Moments later he passed through a low opening and into a bigger, brighter chamber dominated by a large map table. In a corner, a trio of radiomen wearing headsets spoke into microphones, trying not to shout. Several enlisted men moved markers across the large map of Ramree Island covering the table. Here under the concrete and steel, the naval barrage was muffled.

"Shoji!" A man of twenty-three, just a year older than he, made his way over. He was a lieutenant of infantry as well, and had a round, smooth face which made him appear younger, a counterpoint to Shoji's lean features. They shook hands.

Shoji patted the other man's cheek. "When will you begin shaving, Tatsuya-san?"

His friend gave him a deep frown and rubbed his knuckles across Shoji's jawline. "And you are in need of a shave. You look like a beggar, unfit for command. How dare you present yourself at the regimental headquarters in such a condition?"

Shoji smiled. "What will they do, send me to Ramree?"

Tatsuya grinned back with shockingly white teeth and nodded vigorously. "Perhaps make you an infantry officer as added punishment." He tugged on his friend's sleeve. "Come. There is tea, and we have a moment before the briefing begins."

Shoji gratefully followed his friend and helped himself to tea and a hard biscuit, then the two junior officers found a quiet space against a wall and watched. Captain Takahashi, their company commander, was engaged in a heated conversation with another captain and a major on the far side of the table, and other lieutenants like themselves were similarly trying to find an unobtrusive place to stand and be ignored.

"My platoon is down to thirty-nine men," Tatsuya said softly.

Shoji's eyes widened. "What happened? You had close to sixty only a few days ago."

"I lost three during the last bombing run, men caught out in the open when the Lancasters came in on

Wednesday. Three more died at the field hospital from malaria, and another two were killed just before I got here. They were moving from one bunker to another when a round landed in their trench. Fresh recruits, here only a couple of months."

Shoji shook his head. "And the other dozen?"

Tatsuya looked around and lowered his voice. "One of my sergeants took a patrol out to see how far inland the British have advanced, took them down-slope towards Kyaukpnu. Ran into a company of Royal Marines and got chopped to bits. Only a pair of privates made it back, and they said the Brits have moved their artillery up much closer than we thought. Close enough to hit us right here."

"I'm sorry about your men."

Tatsuya shrugged. "At least it's over for them. You and I still have to be here."

Shoji said nothing and sipped his tea.

The room grew quiet a moment later, and a stern-looking man in his forties approached the table, placing his hands flat upon the map of the island. Colonel

Kanichi Nagazawa was bald and narrow, his nose an axe blade beneath dark eyes. He had always reminded Shoji of a falcon, his head movements quick and sharp, eyes catching hold of junior officers and immobilizing them like frightened prey. He made a simple, beckoning hand gesture, and everyone in the room drew close around the table, including the lieutenants along the walls.

"Our position is untenable," he said, his voice low but carrying. "We cannot hold Ramree."

This is not news, Shoji thought.

"We will not surrender. This regiment can still be of use to the Emperor, but to make a stand here is to waste what remains of the 121st. Holding position means British land artillery, ships and aircraft can simply flatten us day after day from a distance without risking troops. For us to go on the offensive is meaningless as well. Though I am confident we would push the enemy back into the sea, it would be a short-lived victory before they landed an even greater force. And there would still be the ongoing problem with offshore batteries and air attack."

Colonel Nagazawa studied the map for a moment, then pointed to the Burmese mainland, close to the eastern edge of Ramree.

"A battalion of the 123rd Infantry Regiment is close by. We will conduct a breakout from our current position," his finger stabbed at a point on the island, "and make a forced march to link up with them." His finger traced a route through an area marked as a vast mangrove swamp joining Ramree Island to mainland Burma. "It is three miles of scattered cover from here to the mangroves, then another twelve miles across until we reach the mainland." He looked up from the map and stared at the men around the table. "We will destroy our vehicles and remaining artillery so as to deny the enemy, and maneuver on foot. We will execute this breakout within the hour, and join the 123rd by zero-six-hundred tomorrow morning."

Glances were exchanged around the room.

"Company commanders," Nagazawa said, "prepare your men to move out by seventeen-hundred hours. Dismissed."

The officers snapped to attention as the colonel left the room, then stood looking at one another for a moment. Prepare a thousand men to move out in an hour? Travel fifteen miles on foot through the night, through a swamp, and accomplish the task by the following morning? British reconnaissance aircraft would most certainly see them moving, and know right where they were going. The enemy would turn their little hike into a killing field.

“You have your orders,” announced the colonel’s executive officer, a major. “See to your commands.” The officers hurried back out into the trench, each man too deep in his own thoughts to notice the naval bombardment had subsided.

It was February 19th, 1945.

2

Ramree Island was a speck of land off the southwestern coast of Burma, strategically valuable in that it had a deep-water port – the town of Kyaukpnu – and an airfield with enough surrounding flat terrain that it could be expanded to accommodate bombers, both aspects making the island attractive to the Japanese. The Emperor's forces captured Ramree as part of their Burma campaign in 1942.

It was a tropical place, dark green and humid and beautiful. For the longest time it had been an active and vibrant location, a critical link to Imperial expansion in the Pacific. Fighters and bombers flew in and out of the airfield on a regular basis, and the port was always crowded with warships and supply freighters. That was back when the Allies were still far away, only just beginning their bloody campaign of island-hopping towards Japan. Back when the garrison had been located in a proper compound in Kyaukpnu, with barracks, a mess hall, hot showers and actual medical facilities.

Despite its beauty, Ramree was far from paradise. Blistering days took their toll, the kind of days where the sky was headache-white, the sun a silver coin overhead. Humidity pressed down like a weight, making time seem to stop, combining with sea salt to destroy machinery and with heat to destroy men. The mosquitoes were virulent with malaria, the snakes numerous and fatal, and in the rainy season the island turned to mud and conspired to drown Ramree's unwelcome visitors in brown sludge. Still, Japan considered the island vital, and kept it garrisoned with the six-thousand men of the 121st Infantry Regiment.

By late 1944, the Allies were folding up the Pacific, and the Imperial Navy was a shadow of its former self. December of that year saw the last Zero depart the airfield, and a final supply ship off-loaded half what it normally delivered to the garrison, departing and leaving the docks empty except for the small fishing boats of the indigenous residents, and a battered frigate which managed to limp to Ramree after being torpedoed, then sank to its gun mounts at wharf side.

The British turned their attention to the island in 1945.

Supported by the battleship HMS Queen Elizabeth, and the light cruiser HMS Phoebe, Royal Marines landed in January expecting a brawl, their commanders not at all convinced they could hold onto a beachhead even if they were able to establish one. Lancaster bombers and Spitfires hammered the garrison while the naval guns shelled the airfield and port, and thousands of marines swarmed out of their landing craft. They met no resistance. The Japanese garrison had pulled out.

Colonel Kanichi Nagazawa was no fool. He had known the landing was inevitable, and was determined to meet the British on his own terms. Under the cover of darkness, he abandoned the port and his coastal positions in advance of the invasion, and fell back to fortifications farther south through the jungle, which he had ordered built months earlier. In this new place, Nagazawa had constructed concrete bunkers and pillboxes, a network of trenches and precisely-measured open killing fields for his artillery and machine guns. Rather than allow the enemy to soften him up by bombardment, he permitted the British to achieve the foothold they sought, drawing them in, then launching attacks of his choosing from the darkness of a jungle his men knew very well. Soon there were British planes burning on that airfield, British barracks and supply dumps in Kyaukpnu being shelled by Japanese artillery, and British soldiers dying in the high grass and palm groves.

The enemy pressed forward, and the Japanese met them with ferocity.

The problem, of course, was that the British could resupply from the sea and Nagazawa could not. Though the 121st gave little ground and the enemy had yet to attempt an assault on the new fortifications, the British were winning a war of attrition and logistics. Their naval guns and aircraft fell into a merciless routine of pounding the Japanese positions day and night. Nagazawa held out this way for over six weeks, and lost five-thousand men in the process. He could hold no longer.

3

The young lieutenant moved quickly from bunker to bunker, passing the word to his men that they would be moving out, ordering them to gather as much food, water and weapons as they could carry. Many were happy to be moving again, especially to be moving away from the trenches and bunkers which were certain to become their graves.

Sergeant Shimizu, his senior enlisted man, followed him closely as the platoon was assembling. "Lieutenant, I looked at our route on the map. Did I hear you correctly that we are to accomplish this march in twelve to thirteen hours?"

"You heard me correctly, Sergeant."

Shimizu shook his head. "Sir, there are no roads, not even a trail marked on that map. It's a swamp, and I know of no one who has actually been through there. In fact the locals…"

Shoji stopped and turned to face him. "Yes?"

"The locals will not even speak about the place. If they are asked, they pretend not to understand and hurry away." There was a time when the natives of Ramree interacted regularly with the occupying Japanese, trading fresh fruit and meat in exchange for batteries and canned goods and clothing. That stopped as the garrison's situation grew more desperate, when the soldiers simply began taking what the locals brought to trade, giving nothing in return and chasing them off with kicks and rifle butts.

"Your point?"

"Sir, with all respect, we have no idea what the terrain will be like. Thirteen hours… The colonel cannot expect –"

Shoji held up a hand. "The colonel has issued his orders, Sergeant, and we will execute them. We have our duty."

Shimizu looked down. "Yes, sir."

The lieutenant put a hand on the man's shoulder. "I don't like it either, Teiko. This will be a hard march. You and I will do all we can to keep our little ducks together and moving, yes?"

The sergeant nodded.

"Make sure they bring as much water as they can carry. More than they think they need."

The man moved off to carry out his assignment, and Shoji returned to the bunker which served as his quarters. He followed his own orders by filling four canteens from a tin bucket, stuffing them into his pack along with some canned rations. He made certain he had his map case, his binoculars, his flashlight and what few medical supplies he had remaining. Then he added in some grenades, checked to ensure his sidearm was loaded and his family sword seated properly on his belt, then shrugged into the pack and donned his helmet. He had no personal items. A photo of his parents and another of Satcheko, as well as her letters, were lost a month ago when a British fire bomb dropped from a Spitfire incinerated his old quarters. Fortunately, he was at a company briefing when the attack came, or he would have followed the photos and letters.

As he emerged from the bunker, the sky was descending through shades of darkening blue and crimson, the sun a swollen blister to the west, hovering above the horizon and turning the sea a fiery orange. At least there were no planes. He inhaled deeply, then moved to join his men.

Lt. Kichida's platoon was near the rear of the column as it stepped off that evening, a winding line of khaki men in double file stretching across flowing grasslands, helmets bobbing in the twilight. Behind them, the engineers had rigged the earth and concrete fortifications with an assortment of explosives and booby traps in anticipation of the inevitable arrival of British ground forces. Their small collection of artillery pieces had already been destroyed, and the few remaining trucks were burning merrily, tires giving off great clouds of stinking black smoke which was hoped might mask their exodus. The skies remained clear, but he knew that wouldn't last long.

With his radioman Aoki close behind him, Shoji Kichida walked alongside the pair of men at the head of 1st Squad; Private Yamada, who had been a fireman on a locomotive before the war, and Private Sasaki, a man several years older than himself, and a chronic complainer and malcontent. Next came Dai the machine-gunner and his loader Riku. Dai was the largest man in the platoon, a fact which earned him the role of gunner since he could more easily bear the weight of the heavy weapon. This was a simple fact experienced by every large infantryman, in every army in the world, since the weapon was invented. Riku trudged beside him laden with layer upon layer of belted ammunition, his head and back bowed under the burden.

Yoichi, the squad prankster, followed Riku and gently prodded his behind with a stick, making soft donkey noises until Sgt. Shimizu slapped the back of his helmet and told him to stop. Yoichi only grinned wider, nudging his friend Matsuda, the young fisherman. The rest trailed after, men he knew, some better than others, some whom he liked better than others, but all his responsibility.

The sun was crouched where the sea met the sky, a ball of red which seemed to hover for a minute before it slipped down and out of sight. Red clouds trailed overhead as the gentle, downward slope of the fields eased towards nightfall. Insects whirred and jumped in the high grasses, and already bats were arriving from the jungle to swoop in low and fast to snatch them up, small black blurs against the purple sky.

Judging by the time and the pace the column was keeping, Shoji estimated that the head of the column would be arriving at the edge of the swamp at any moment. Everything would slow down and back up as men started in, leaving the column and especially Shoji's platoon far in the back, exposed in the open. A moment later that was exactly what happened, men coming to an abrupt halt, many bumping into the soldier in front of them and cursing.

Shoji watched the skies. If the British hadn't noticed the long line of men leaving the fortifications, their attention would surely be drawn by the fires from the trucks. He summoned Sgt. Shimizu.

"Order the men to use the grass for concealment."

The sergeant nodded, and together he and Shoji moved back down the line, ensuring that everyone got down and out of sight in the tall grass. The platoon in front of them saw what they were doing, and quickly followed suit. It had a ripple effect, and within minutes the column was dropping out of sight from back to front.

The radio squealed, and Captain Takahashi's voice came across. "What the hell is going on back there? Get those men on their feet and ready to move!"

Shoji stood from his crouch and ordered his men out of hiding and back into column formation, his cheeks red. The rest of the column did the same. They had all nearly returned to their original, standing double lines when the drone of engines came to them from the east. All eyes turned towards the sound. Infantrymen are intimately attuned to the sound and behavior of aircraft, despising them above all other weapons. They quickly made out the cluster of shapes approaching in the evening sky.

"Take cover!" Shoji yelled, as every man dove for the high grass.

A Lancaster bomber flanked by a pair of Spitfires roared in low, clumps of small black shapes dropping from its belly. In seconds the grasslands erupted in sound, in clouds of earth and fire and whizzing steel fragments. Bits of metal cut through the grass and men screamed, just as the two spitfires opened up and strafed the column with their wing-mounted guns. They sounded like giant zippers, the rounds chopping into dirt and flesh in long twin lines before the planes growled past in a blur.

Aoki's radio was chattering somewhere in the grass, but Shoji couldn't see him, his own body pressed flat as he held onto his helmet with both hands. Someone was screaming. He hoped it wasn't him.

The fighters turned and came in for another pass, taking the column lengthwise this time, raking it with fire all the way to the front, where men had begun to break formation and were running scattered into the shelter of the mangrove trees. Bodies tumbled face-down in the grass, helmets and weapons flying as still more men leaped over their fallen comrades, racing for cover, unconcerned with the shouts of officers or NCOs, wanting only to get out of sight. A few stopped and fired their rifles at the departing planes, which banked away and headed out of sight over the treetops, their guns dry.

Then came the thunder of naval guns, followed by high-pitched whistles, and the smaller crack of field artillery far to their rear. Shoji climbed to his feet and started barking for Sgt. Shimizu to get the men up, get them moving before they were annihilated. All along the column officers were doing the same, urging their men forward, the orderly column lost as they ran their men down the hillside in frantic bands.

More explosions, much larger than the bombs from the Lancasters, tore apart the terrain, dirt and debris and pieces of men blown out in wide circles. The shells landed far to the sides, behind them, some closer, some upon the groups of men themselves as the British worked to find their range and accuracy. Shoji was running now, his men behind him and his sergeant bringing up the rear. In the distance was a dark line of foliage, the edge of the swamp, clusters of tiny, running shapes passing into it from the fields. That was where he led them, his legs and arms pumping.

Shells screamed out of the sky all around them, cratering the hillside, blowing apart clumps of trees. He saw a man in front of him stumble, suddenly without a head, then collapse onto his chest with his arms limp at his sides. He ran past a boy lying shrieking in the grass and trying to hold his intestines in his belly. Still the shells fell like rain, ahead, behind, among them.

Shoji didn't know if his men were still with him, his heart racing with panic, afraid to stop to look back. It was weak and wrong, but he couldn't help it. All he wanted was the trees, the trees, to get out of the open, off this hillside, to run, run, run.

A blast close to his right lifted him into the air and then slammed him to earth. Painful white blossoms filled his eyes, and his breath went out with a thumping wheeze. He tried to draw in, lips opening and closing like a fish, but there was no air.

This is death, he thought. It hurts.

Another blast and a scream and something wet spattered across his face, across the lenses of his eyeglasses, somehow unbroken. His lips moved, and he pawed helplessly at the grass, straining to draw breath, curled on his side. The ground jumped with a ripple of impacts, making him bounce, and he heard deadly whispers of shrapnel cutting through the air a foot over his head. Men were yelling and wailing, and he still couldn't breathe.

A red shadow appeared above him, gripping him by his combat harness and hauling him to his feet. Shoji managed a tiny gasp, feeling his lungs tremble, then feeling himself dragged, stumbling through the grass as someone pulled at him. Another wheeze, his chest burning, then another, sucking in sweet bursts of air. He tore his bloody eyeglasses off his face to see Cpl. Aoki hauling him along amid a cluster of running men, the radio on his back a shattered wreck of dangling metal and sparking wires. Shoji allowed himself to be pulled, trying to regain his feet and his breath at the same time. Geysers of earth and grass erupted around them as shells landed, the explosions battering them, bodies spinning through the air to the right and left.

How long have we been running, Shoji wondered? Where are the trees?

And then the trees appeared, a snaking line of red and black mangroves at the base of the hillside, roots high and arching, reaching for the water beyond. From within the tree line came the splashing and yelling of men as they blundered into the darkness, tripping and falling, trying to distance themselves from the murderous fire. Shoji staggered into water up to his knees, nearly falling, hugging a mangrove trunk to keep from going down, Aoki still tugging on him.

There was the high-pitched shriek, a blast of red-white heat and pain, and Shoji was ripped from the tree and thrown onto his back in the water. He swallowed a mouthful, choked and began to thrash with his arms and legs, a root digging sharply into his back. He clawed his way up, sitting, gasping for air and wiping water and mud from his eyes.

Before him, a round from the British battleship had created a twenty foot clearing, the surrounding trees shattered, and burning leaves drifting down to hiss in the water. Pieces of men floated on the surface. Shoji felt his forehead stinging, wiped at it, his fingers coming away bloody. He wiggled them and stared at them, then noticed Cpl. Aoki's left hand still gripping his combat harness, dangling from his chest, ending in a ragged red stump.

Where was the rest of him? Should he call for him?

"Lieutenant! Lieutenant!"

Shoji looked up to see Dai his machine-gunner twenty feet away in the trees, Riku still beside him.

"Lieutenant!" Dai yelled again.

Shoji blinked, still disoriented from the blast, and for a moment unsure of what he was doing here. Then he noticed the hand again and tore it away in disgust, pitching it into the watery crater and crawling to his feet. He stumbled over to Dai and Riku. Shells were exploding around them in the swamp, and on the hillside to their rear.

"Where is everyone?" He had to shout for the men to hear him.

"I saw Sgt. Shimizu!" Dai pointed deeper into the swamp. "A few others. Everyone is all mixed up!"

Shoji nodded and wiped again as the cut on his forehead dripped into his eyes. He had lost his glasses. "Follow me," he yelled, heading into the gloom of the swamp with his men close behind, heading towards the noise of others, in water up to his knees, the mud below pulling at his boots.

4

Private Fairweather was forward in the patrol boat, one of a six man crew of Royal Marines. A gunner's assistant, his job was to feed belts of .50 caliber ammo to the heavy machinegun mounted in a small, open turret in the bow. At the moment he was seated on a bench to the rear of the turret, his back pressed against the armored plate partition shielding the motor launch operator, both hands gripping the seat between his thighs as the boat pounded over the waves. The bow rose and slammed back down, making his teeth click together, and causing his stomach to leap with every rise and fall.

He didn't want to be sick again. This was his first week in combat, and already he had thrown up on the boat half a dozen times. It wasn't making him popular with the crew. Bad enough that he was the newest man on board, freshly arrived from training in England.

Salt spray feathered back from the bow, and he turned his face and squinted away from it. Ramree was off to port, a long, hilly lump in a darkening blue sea, crowned with palms and dark green like an unpolished emerald. His stomach lurched and his gorge rose, and for a moment he wished he was ashore with his rifle, unmoving land beneath his boots, but the thought quickly passed. He had seen the marines being brought back from Ramree, maimed and torn, gaunt and exhausted and suffering from malaria. And he had seen the bags of the dead, too. No, better to vomit every day and endure the ridicule of his mates than end up like that. The island was said to be swarming with ten thousand bloodthirsty Japanese, each one jabbering and screaming to cut off an Englishman's head with their samurai swords, scoop out the brains and use the skull as a bowl for their rice wine. He knew he'd have to go ashore eventually, but better later than now.

A trio of planes roared overhead in formation, heading towards the island. He was too far away to see the bomber at their center drop its load, but he heard the big naval guns a few minutes later as they began hammering the island. The sergeant said a large Japanese force was on the move, and with a little luck the shells would find their mark. He hoped so. The more Japs the artillery killed, the fewer he would have to face when the orders came for Private Fairweather of Dunham, England to hit the beach.

Kill them all, he wished, watching as smoke rose from the island in columns.

Forward in the .50 cal turret, nestled down low with only the top of his helmet showing, Specialist Browne stretched his arms up over his head and let out a great yawn which Fairweather could hear even over the hull slapping on the surface. Browne, Fairweather's immediate boss, wasn't a bad sort. He took the time to teach him things when it was quiet, and he never said anything unkind when the private got sick, though he would roll his eyes and tell him to clean it up. But he could be a prick if Fairweather was slow to reload the weapon, or tried to feed the rounds backwards as he had on his second day in the boat. On that day, reports had come in that Japanese had been spotted moving through the tree line along the western edge of Ramree, and Fairweather's boat had raced to the spot to pour .50 caliber fire into the jungle. The fifty had banged away until the bolt snapped open and empty. Shaken by the sudden dash of the patrol boat and the deafening clatter of the heavy machinegun, he hurried and tripped, dropping the belt of ammo. When he scrambled to his feet and began feeding the belt to the gunner's weapon, the bullets had been facing backwards. Browne screamed, spit flying from his lips as he threatened to throw Fairweather overboard if he didn't unfuck himself right bloody now!

It was hard to believe that four weeks ago he had been in England, looking proper in a clean, crisp uniform, boarding a train in Dunham with his unit, bound for a Southhampton freighter. His mother and father were on the platform to see him off, his mum crying and telling him to be careful, to remember to write. Father was stoic and stiff with a firm handshake and a "Make us proud, son," but his eyes were filled with worry. A month later he was on the other side of the world, patrolling off an island no one had ever heard of, looking for an enemy he had yet to see.

Someone rapped their knuckles on Fairweather's helmet, startling him and making him look back. Sergeant Bremer was leaning over the armored partition.

"Fifteen minutes to station," he yelled. "Make sure Browne's awake."

Fairweather nodded.

The sergeant leveled a big finger at him. "And don't even think of heaving once we get there. You got anything to get rid of, do it now."

Fairweather flushed and turned away. He *did* feel like heaving, but there was nothing left in his stomach except for watery bile. For an instant he imagined standing and puking right in Bremer's face. It made him smile a little.

The motor launch began a long, left curve around Ramree's southern tip, turning in towards the island, the great stretch of mainland Burma coming into view beyond it. The island sat about fifteen miles off Burma's coast, the mainland a soft dark line in the distance. Night was falling, and on this side of Ramree it was darker, the last hint of sunlight blocked by the island. Within minutes a second patrol boat appeared to starboard. It was identical to his own, and assigned, as his boat was, to the HMS Phoebe to their rear which right now was pouring fire onto the island. Both launches were on the same heading, their patrol area the most likely point for a Japanese withdrawal.

The island's coastline became more defined as they drew nearer, the smear of green and black slowly turning into individual trees and tangled canopy. A strip of white beach met the sea. Ahead he could see the island was joined to the larger land mass by a low strip of dense, twisted trees, the swamp his sergeant had spoken about. Fairweather's boat began to slow, and the launch off to the right did the same, taking up position a hundred yards off.

Now the thumping of the bow was replaced by a steady, up and down swell as they continued to close, and Fairweather's stomach began to feel better. He unsnapped the latches of the ammo locker and started straightening the belts inside where they had been tossed about by the high speed, telling himself over and over to move quickly but carefully when the time came, to remember his training and feed the belts without delay into the .50 when Browne called out. And not to puke.

The ammo ready, he lifted his binoculars and started his second job, spotting the shoreline for targets. The sergeant said the Japanese would be moving into that swamp, and the crew's orders were to watch the trees and open up on anyone they saw. Fairweather swallowed hard, hoping he would see them before they spotted his motor launch. If Browne's heavy machinegun could reach the trees, then the Japanese guns could also reach the patrol boat. After several tense minutes of watching, his heartbeat pounding in his ears like a blacksmith's hammer, he shook his head. He was being stupid. Soon it would be too dark to even see the island, and impossible for the enemy to spot his tiny boat bobbing out here on a dark sea.

"Phoebe and Queen Elizabeth are coming up on our stern," Bremer announced to the crew. Both the cruiser and the much bigger battleship had their guns elevated towards Ramree, still firing as the vessels cut through the water at a stately pace, the reports of each shot rumbling over the waves. Pieces of jungle and pillars of smoke rose after each hit, and as Fairweather continued to watch the trees, he took a moment to thank God for not making him Japanese.

5

Shoji Kichida was born to rice farmers outside Hokkaido, raised in a small village among the paddies of stepped hillsides. A simple life, and one which would have suited him fine. It was not to be. A talent for engineering revealed itself in him at an early age. He seemed to have a natural understanding of how mechanical devices functioned, how to take them apart and put them back together, and how to construct mechanisms which worked.

At age twelve he understood that the old water wheel near his home, designed to bring water up from a stream and dump it into a higher, primary rice paddy, was well past its prime and inefficient. Using bamboo and a design he sketched out on rice paper, he built a new one which was not only sturdier, but carried more water, more quickly. It earned him the attention and admiration of the village. Soon he was redesigning the axles of ox carts, building chicken and pig sheds which were stronger and required less wood, and even dreamed up and constructed a rickshaw, giving rides to village children, delighting them and their parents alike. By his middle teens he was being consulted by villagers for his opinion on larger projects like homes, and when he was fourteen the elder of a neighboring village presented himself at his parent's home and asked if Shoji would design a small house for his daughter and her husband-to-be.

In school, his test and aptitude scores brought him to the attention of administrators in the rural education system, and at seventeen Shoji found himself bound for university, the first from his village – and his family – to achieve such an honor. It was a source of great pride for his parents, and for Satcheko. She had been there with his parents to see him off at the train, quietly holding her emotions in check, giving him a tender kiss on the cheek and a long look with her dark eyes, softly telling him she would be waiting.

A little over one year into his studies, Shoji was informed that the Emperor required him to defend the homeland. He was pulled from university, quickly sworn into military service and transitioned to officer's school. He hoped, even expected to enter the engineer corps. Would it not be foolish for him to serve otherwise? His father and Satcheko made the long trip to see him graduate as a nineteen-year-old 2nd lieutenant. She told him how handsome he looked in his uniform, and allowed him to hold her close while she whispered in his ear, pledging herself to him. His father was proud but somber, and presented him with the family sword, a beautiful, slightly curved katana in a black lacquer sheath. It was over two-hundred years old, and by tradition Shoji, like many young Japanese men, was expected to carry the weapon to war as his ancestors had done. He accepted the humbling gift quietly, with his head bowed, promising his father he would not dishonor him.

The new graduates received their assignments that evening. He was not assigned to the engineer corps. The following morning Shoji was shipped out to begin the harsh training of an infantry officer.

He considered himself fortunate to have survived three years of jungle warfare. His infantry command training was abbreviated out of a desperate need for field leaders, and he was quickly thrown into Burma as a green, terrified 2nd lieutenant. For him, the war began on his third day in the jungle, when a British patrol ambushed his column, killing a dozen men including the commanding captain and the other two officers before fading back into the greenery. A very frightened Lt. Kichida suddenly found himself in command of over a hundred men, each one more experienced than he. They were disciplined enough to wait for and obey the directives of an officer, depending upon him to make the right decisions and not get them killed. He couldn't remember the details of their retreat, had only vague memories of hit-and-run firefights among the dense foliage. And yet he marched his men back into friendly lines with only two more wounded and none killed. He very clearly remembered handing the unit off to a senior officer, then ducking behind a medical tent where he spent the next twenty minutes vomiting and shaking.

Shoji would not see the island until late 1944. By then had been promoted to full lieutenant, a veteran numbed by an endless parade of death, each scene more grisly than the one before. He lost men, he lost friends, he killed the enemy, he did his duty. But he grew hollow and tired, and never as tired as he felt at this very moment.

They were gathered around a rotted stump, a group of officers considerably fewer in number than had been at the briefing in the bunker. Had that only been this afternoon, he wondered? It felt like weeks ago. Ocean breezes did not penetrate into the swamp, stopping short at the tree line, leaving the mangroves close and humid, men sticky and wheezing in the hot, damp air. Shirts not already soaked from the water were dark with sweat, and cloth caps were wet and crusting with white rings of salt. Mosquitoes descended from the dark canopy to feed upon them all.

Someone placed a wooden ammo crate on the stump as an impromptu table, and another pointed a hooded flashlight at the map being spread out upon it, only to be told sharply to turn it off, the moonlight would suffice. Shoji thought there was precious little of that dripping through the canopy. Colonel Nagazawa was at the ammo crate, examining the terrain lines while the others stood silent, the older man removing his cap to wipe a palm over his shaved head. Neither the major or Shoji's commanding officer Captain Takahashi was present, the major having been killed during the run for the trees, Takahashi missing and presumed dead.

The shelling ceased shortly after the last man staggered into the concealment of the mangroves. Now, less than a mile into the swamp and a quarter of the regiment scattered, the officers were standing in water up to their waists. This was a tidal swamp, and it had risen steadily all through the sunset. As an infantryman and a rice farmer, Shoji knew little about tides, but enough to know that the deeper water would slow their movement to a crawl, to say nothing of the sucking gray mud beneath it. He looked around for Tatsuya, not seeing him, and whispered an inquiry to a young officer beside him. The other man only shrugged.

"This will be our line of advance," the colonel said, tracing his finger slowly across the map. Shoji saw only a blur. He could distinguish faces well enough, but only because he knew most of them. Without his glasses, reading was impossible. He had already tried to look at his compass, but found it fuzzy as well. For that reason, he prayed he would not be asked to take the point.

Nagazawa looked at the men around him. "I have sent several officers and sergeants out in an attempt to collect our missing troops back to the column. They will have to rejoin us on the move."

That must be where Tatsuya was, Shoji thought. He hoped.

"We have much distance to travel, and the enemy will resume shelling as soon as their gun tubes cool and the bombers have refueled and reloaded." His eyes narrowed and his lips drew thin. "I will not tolerate the break in discipline, the chaos I saw on the hillside. You will control your men and keep order within your formations."

The young officers gave short bows, ashamed.

"Lt. Masato, your platoon will take point. Move them up, we step off in ten minutes." He held up a finger. "We are under strict light and noise discipline. No lights except for the point officer, and there will be no smoking." He looked at Masato, who stood rigidly. "You and your compass had best stay close to your point man, Lieutenant. The enemy will be waiting for us to appear at the shoreline, so do not lead the column astray."

Masato bowed and barked a quick, "Hai!" before wading off to assemble his men. Nagazawa gave out the order of march, and Shoji learned his platoon would be third from the front. As he left the meeting to find Sergeant Shimizu, his boots crunched on oysters nestled in the muddy bottom. A treat he would have enjoyed under normal circumstances, he suspected these oysters would be wretched, immersed in the overly-salty, fetid mud, fit only for long-legged cranes.

A minute after leaving the group, Shoji tripped over an exposed root and went face first into the water, coming up coughing an instant later. He wiped at his eyes and looked around at the darkness, but could discern no human figures, only the twisted shapes of mangroves. He stopped. How could he have become lost in less than a minute? He cursed losing his glasses, leaned a palm on a tree trunk and began a slow circle, high-stepping over roots and squinting into the darkness. Something scuttled across the back of his hand and he jerked it away, looking to see what it was, spotting a small dark shape disappearing into a crook of the tree. Probably a crab. He had seen them swarming over the bases of the mangroves when it was still light. Just a crab.

"Lieutenant." A whisper from somewhere close in front of him. "Over here."

Shoji stepped away from the tree, wading towards the voice, and a moment later made out Sgt. Shimizu in the thin moonlight. He was happy to see the man, and the sergeant either hadn't noticed his officer was lost or was at least polite enough not to show it. Shoji gave him

Nagazawa's orders, then inquired about the platoon. Shimizu had already been gathering strays without being told, and reported only nine of the fifty missing. He was able to account for five as shelling casualties, and Shoji told him about Aoki the radioman. That left three unaccounted-for. Shoji peered around at the darkness.

"They're probably dead, sir," said Shimizu. "Either on the hillside or in here. No way we'll find the bodies."

"And if they're simply wounded?" Shoji asked.

Shimizu said nothing.

The lieutenant knew his sergeant had no answer, and there was nothing to be done. "Assemble the men and move them up."

The sergeant turned and waded into the darkness. There were no calls of "Get on your feet!" Everyone was already standing. Sitting down meant drowning. Several minutes later the platoon was in a rough line, angling in towards other voices. Getting them into place in the formation was a farce, as hundreds of figures stumbled and fell and bumped into each other, mistaking one unit for another in the darkness. Without lights, it was an impossible task. Yet eventually the column was assembled and began moving forward. Instead of Nagazawa's directive for ten minutes, it took an hour.

By ten o'clock that night, only four hours since they entered the tree line, the column advanced a single mile. The mud got worse as they moved deeper in, bogging down men, pulling off boots, making each step an effort. The line of soldiers often seemed not to move at all, a snake of helmeted shadows taking a forward step every few minutes, packed in closely. The heat weighed down on them all, heavier than their packs and weapons, and with it came clouds of mosquitoes so thick at times they blotted out the weak strands of moonlight coming through the branches. Those who were able dug spare shirts and towels out of their gear, wrapping them about their faces and necks to ward off the bloodthirsty insects, while others slapped and swore and slapped some more, but it made little difference. No one had any repellant – on Ramree it got used up quickly, and the garrison hadn't been re-supplied in months. Before long every man's face was swollen, lumpy and irritated.

Shoji was trudging beside Dai and Riku, the larger man with the machinegun across his shoulders, wrists draped loosely over the weapon, his loader wheezing like an asthmatic under the weight of the ammo belts. No one spoke, and Shoji let his mind drift back to his village.

It would be cold there now, the paddies crusted with a thin film of ice, the grass brown and stiff, brisk winds sliding across the steep hillsides. Maybe there would be snow. The house would be warm, his father keeping a small fire banked against the chill, his mother working quietly preparing cabbage and rice, perhaps brewing a pot of tea. Satcheko would be with them, re-reading the last letters he had been able to send, months ago now. They would gather near the hearth and listen to the wind groaning through the eaves of the little house, Satcheko's sweet voice filling the room. She would skip over the personal parts, the places where he told her how he longed to touch her fine, black hair, to cup her beautiful face in his hands and kiss her full lips. Would she also pass over the part where he told her he loved her, that he wanted only to return to a simple life and make her the wife of a rice farmer? Probably. Satcheko was quite reserved, though not when they were alone together.

You assume she has waited for you, announced a voice, the unpleasant one which had grown in his head over the recent years. *It has been a long, long time. She is young and beautiful, and does not even know if you are alive or dead. Perhaps she shares a bed with Hisao, the tailor's son?*

Shut up, he told the voice. As usual it defied him.

Is she still alive? Are any of them? Hokkaido is not far away, and surely the American bombers have been hitting it. Perhaps one of them wandered before dropping its payload? The village is likely little more than a crater on the hillside, your family and lovely Satcheko buried at the bottom.

Though he commanded the voice to be silent, in truth he could not argue with it. What it said was more than possible, and he simply didn't know. Though he had written and sent numerous letters, he had not received mail in nine months. Shoji no longer considered himself an optimist. Hope was the first casualty of war, and he was no exception. He could have been philosophical about it, thinking on karma and the mysteries of fate, but he found the best he could muster was a cold resignation. He supposed it was despair, though he dared not speak the word, and would not dishonor his family by showing it. If they were dead, if Satcheko was dead and he somehow made it home to learn this terrible truth, he knew it would destroy him. But not here. Not yet. There were others depending upon him. He would allow his soul to die later.

Riku suddenly cried out and shrugged his ammo belts off his shoulders and into the water, twisting and dancing as well as the mud would allow, clawing and slapping frantically at his neck, his chest, his face. A rising moan of panic came from him, and Shoji immediately shoved past the big gunner to reach the boy. Riku flapped his arms and kept slapping as he grunted and sobbed.

Shoji gripped the boy by the shoulders and hissed for him to be quiet, but Riku pulled away, clawing at his neck. Shoji felt a tingle on both hands, followed by painful pinpricks, and pinched at what he felt there.

Ants. Black, biting ants. Riku must have brushed against a tree trunk and disturbed a cluster of them, a tiny army marching up or down the bark in its own military columns. Shoji felt the tingling under his sleeves, and he grabbed the boy by the shoulders again and forced him down into the water, submerging himself as well, going all the way under. The tingle stopped at once as the ants quickly drowned, and Riku stopped thrashing, suddenly understanding and staying under with his officer as long as he could hold his breath. When they came up together in a whoosh, Dai and several others were standing around looking concerned.

Shoji held Riku's shoulders for a long moment, looking into his eyes, murmuring to him. Riku nodded and thanked his lieutenant.

"Ants," Shoji said to the gathered men. "Don't rub against the trees." He looked at Riku and pointed at the water. "I want every ammo belt recovered." Then he moved away to find the head of his platoon.

They marched for another hour before word was passed through the column calling a fifteen minute break.

Aching men groaned in agreement, but their pleasure soon evaporated when they realized there was no place to sit. Most quickly moved back to back and leaned against each other, arms heavy and barely able to hold their rifles above the surface of the water. A few decided to take their chances and leaned against the mangroves after inspecting them for ants. Before any of the NCOs could put a stop to it, the soldiers downed half the water in their canteens.

His thigh muscles burning from the exertion, Shoji made a complete circuit of his platoon, checking on every man, cautioning them to conserve their water, to keep their weapons dry, to stay on their feet. He found a trio of men using their bayonets in an attempt to open oysters, and ordered them to stop, to drop them back in the water. A brief visit with Matsuda, the young fisherman, revealed the boy was beginning to display symptoms of malaria. Feverish and shaking, he complained of both chills and sweats. Shoji knew few men in the regiment still had quinine tablets to drop in their drinking water – he had finished his own personal supply over a week ago – and was surprised more men weren't presenting symptoms. He told the boy to be strong, then quietly told Yoichi, Matsuda's friend, to keep an eye on him and report if he appeared to be getting worse. As he slogged away, Shoji sighed, knowing he would be able to do nothing if and when that report came in. It had just been the right thing to say.

The lieutenant was three-quarters of the way around the platoon when he smelled cigarette smoke. He looked around sharply. "Who is that?"

The soldiers said nothing.

"Who is smoking?" he demanded. Still no one spoke, but eyes turned towards the front of the platoon. Shoji picked up his weary knees and stomped through the mud and water as quickly as he could. His splashing alerted the offender, and up ahead he saw the red tip of a cigarette being flicked off into the darkness. Shoji marked the spot and advanced until he reached the approximate point from where the butt and been pitched. He wasn't even a little surprised to see Sasaki, the older man, the malcontent.

"What were my orders?" Shoji said tightly.

Sasaki looked at him, and Shoji could swear he saw a smirk in the gloom. "About what…sir?"

"Smoking."

"I wasn't smoking, Lieutenant."

"Liar! You reek of it." Shoji pointed to Yamada, standing next to Sasaki. "Was he smoking?"

Sasaki shot a hard look at Yamada, who simply looked down, then he looked back at his officer. This time there was no doubt he was smiling.

"Give them to me," Shoji said, holding out a palm.

Sasaki paused for a moment, then slowly pulled a crumpled pack out of a breast pocket and slapped it into Shoji's hand. The lieutenant immediately submerged the pack, held it under for a full minute while he glared silently at the solder, then handed it back. Tobacco slime oozed out of the open end.

"No lights. No smoking. Do you understand, Private?"

The older man's smirk went away, but his eyes were hard and challenging. "Yes, *sir.*"

Shoji stomped away, knowing the man was sending one obscene gesture or another at his back. Had his platoon been leading the column, he would have ordered Sasaki to walk point as punishment. But they weren't, and besides, the man would probably either run off or lead them into an ambush. He sighed and finished inspecting his men, and then the break was over and it was time to step off again.

The British ships began their bombardment five minutes later.

6

It started with the Queen Elizabeth's 15" guns, quickly joined by her 6" tubes, ripples of blinding white flashes to their rear, followed by waves of crashing sound. Sgt. Bremer barked at Fairweather to stop gawking and look forward, to preserve his night vision, but it was several moments before the young man could take his eyes off the light show as the battleship began dropping 381mm shells on the swamp. He faced forward and rubbed his fists into his eyes. The sergeant was right. He couldn't see a thing.

Minutes later the Phoebe joined in with her batteries of 5" guns, the rounds arcing overhead and sounding like ripping fabric. Ahead, what had been blackness only moments ago was lit by a series of red and white flashes as the shells began landing in the swamp. Trees were silhouetted in black against the explosions, which tracked slowly from left to right. At this distance, the sound of the impacts was muffled, rolling across the water like distant thunder. The radio crackled with faint voices behind him

They had been idling, holding position for hours, but now the engines of the patrol boat rumbled to life. Fairweather felt the deck vibrate beneath his boots as the boat nudged forward over the calm seas, closing on the island.

"Command thinks the shelling might scatter them, force some to the shoreline," called Bremer. "We're getting in close in case they do. Look sharp, Browne. Fire on any movement."

In the gun turret, a hand rose to give a thumbs-up.

Both warships fired simultaneously, and as the blasts rippled among the trees, Fairweather was once again thankful he was on water instead of land. The next salvo was a mixture of star clusters and flares. The clusters were white fireworks which turned the strip of land before them into a surreal landscape of black and white. The flares, intensely-burning white lights drifting slowly to earth on parachutes, illuminated the area within the tree line, but really succeeded only in creating a dizzy mix of darkness and light. Fairweather watched, the boat close enough now that he didn't need his binoculars, but couldn't distinguish real movement from flare-induced shadow. He swore under his breath. A company could be moving through there and he wouldn't know the difference.

Once the patrol boat was within fifty yards of the shore it slowed, and Bremer ordered the engines cut. After a short forward drift the craft settled and rocked softly from side to side. Off to the right, their sister boat did the same.

Fairweather gauged the distance between himself and the shore. Fifty yards was awfully close, certainly within rifle range. He retrieved his sub machinegun from a locker, checked to see that it was armed and safe, then slung it across his chest. He wondered if it could reach the trees. He knew the 7.7mm rifle the Japanese carried could reach him easily, and without realizing he was doing it, he shuffled sideways until the steel enclosure of

Browne's turret was between him and the shore. Now he was at least somewhat shielded from the hips down.

"You're learning," said Sgt. Bremer. Fairweather turned to see the older man watching him, and received a nod. He looked forward again, relieved. At least he had done something right.

It didn't take long before the flares went out, and the big ships fired more, intermingling them with the live rounds. Explosions marched up and down the swamp, left to right and back again, some close enough to the shoreline that Fairweather saw fragmented trees blown into the water, some far enough away that he wondered if they might have even overshot. The sergeant said the swamp was only a mile wide in most places.

He watched as the night was lit by a hellish light, wondering how anyone could possibly survive that.

7

They don't know where we are, Shoji thought. They don't know what this place is like, and assume we've made it farther along. The lieutenant was standing beside Yamada, the locomotive fireman, watching the British tear hell out of the swamp far ahead of them. Brilliant flashes split the darkness, followed by a bloom of fire and the crunch of an explosion, all seen behind a twisted, black curtain of mangroves. Nothing landed too close to the column, and most of it was far ahead or to the sides.

Colonel Nagazawa had ordered the regiment to halt and hold position, to let the enemy waste his ordnance on the swamp, guessing at their location. It was a wise tactic. Yet after close to an hour of standing and watching, Shoji began to wonder if the British had an unlimited supply of rounds. Would it never end? He was thankful for the inaccuracy of the naval guns, but even more so for the darkness. The enemy apparently didn't have any night-capable aircraft in the area, or they would have been overhead, using the light from the flares to spot for the bombers, which most certainly *were* night-capable. But someone on the other side must have decided not to bother sending out the bombers if they couldn't get a fix on the target. Shoji knew that would change in the daylight.

Another fifteen minutes saw the end of the bombardment, and once the colonel was satisfied it was truly over, he ordered the column forward again. It was well past midnight, and they were clearly not going to meet his rigid travel schedule. As the night descended once more, so too came the resumption of an achingly slow forward advance, a step every few minutes as men heaved their boots against the mud, wading waist deep and aching to sit and rest their legs, bumping into the man in front of them and having packs shoved back at them in annoyance. Although the water felt a little cooler, it brought no relief from the hot, heavy air, and exhausted men grumbled and snapped at one another as they plodded through the darkness, NCOs barking at them to be quiet.

Shoji tried repeatedly to return to the cool pleasures of his village, but the swamp would have none of it. The biting ants returned with a vengeance, swarming across low-hanging branches which the men were forced to push through, attacking exposed flesh and getting under uniforms. The soldiers plunged themselves again and again into the foul water to escape the ants, trying to keep their rifles above the surface. After a while they stopped trying, wanting only to drown the painful insects, not caring that whatever they carried was being water-logged. Not that it mattered, there was no one to shoot at. Most reasoned that the British were too smart to follow them into this hell on foot, remaining comfortably out on their boats, laughing as the shells did the work for them.

The ant bites stung long after the creatures drowned, then began to itch. Scratching only inflamed them, causing more pain. Shoji was as bitten-up as the rest, covered in ant and mosquito welts, gritting his teeth and forcing himself not to scratch, even though the itching was maddening.

Men tripped over submerged roots and fell face first into the water. The mud sucked off boots, forcing men to go on barefoot, cutting their soles on jagged oyster shells. Some tried to eat on the move, dropping tins of rations or mess kits and losing them in the water. Another man lost his rifle, and his angry sergeant slapped him in the head so many times his helmet came off and sank as well. An ammo crate was dropped and quickly went to the bottom. In the darkness, none of it could be recovered.

Shoji stayed close to his men, making constant inquiries about how they were feeling, encouraging them, cajoling them. Matsuda was now complaining of a headache and nausea, Yoichi helping him along and carrying the boy's pack and rifle for him. Sasaki was complaining of fever and abdominal pain, but since whining was a normal state for him, his complaints went ignored. Shoji was more concerned with the two men lugging a crate of mortar shells between them. Their palms were raw and bloody from the rubbing of the rope handles, and the salt water turned the wounds into an unbearable burning. The lieutenant looked for a medic, couldn't find one, then canvassed the men until he found four handkerchiefs with which to bind their hands, assigning the mortar crate duty to two other men.

Water penetrated Shoji's wristwatch, stopping it, and he could only guess that it was one or two in the morning when there was a scream behind him, somewhere back in his platoon. This was followed by the excited voices of men, followed by more screams from the same area, and then again from in front of his unit. Shoji high-stepped at the mud and water and made his way back to the commotion. He saw Colonel Nagazawa closing from the other direction, getting there first, demanding to know who was breaking silence discipline.

A cluster of men were slapping and brushing at their uniforms, at each other's backs and shoulders. Others were submerging themselves, and all were on the edge of panic. Nagazawa covered a flashlight with a palm and snapped it on, allowing a slit of light out. He shone it on the men.

Shoji saw it at once, scuttling up over a soldier's shoulder and onto his neck, a hairy, cobalt blue spider the size of his own hand. It bit, and the man cried out, punching at the creature, which only raced across his chest and around to his back.

"They're everywhere!" shrieked a man, tearing off his pack and dropping it into the water, trying to rip off his uniform blouse. In the narrow flashlight beam Shoji could see a dark, swollen bite on the man's left cheek, seeming to grow larger as he watched, misshaping the man's face. The soldier's fingertips brushed the swelling and he cried out, then stumbled, his eyes rolling upwards as he gasped and collapsed with a splash.

They did seem to be everywhere, running over men and biting repeatedly, caught in bare hands which they then sank their fangs into, being thrown into the darkness or crushed. Shoji saw more of them dropping from the canopy above, inkblots of eight-legged venom leaping down from the trees. He felt something land on his cap, and a moment later it raced across his face. Shoji cried out and batted it away into the water.

Nagazawa was waving his arms. “Move forward! Forward! Clear the area!”

Men slogged ahead as fast as they could, still ditching equipment and trying to crush the spiders on themselves and each other. The colonel ordered the men following to swing wide of the area, uncovering his flashlight and shining the full beam into the canopy and panning it around.

There were hundreds of tarantulas. Thousands perhaps, big and sprinting along the mangrove branches, scuttling over broad leaves, running up and down the trunks. A few continued to drop, but they landed only in the water as the men moved out of the breeding ground. Nagazawa himself was bitten on the neck before he managed to get clear, and within sixty seconds a pair of junior officers was holding the man up between them as the colonel’s neck swelled and he began to struggle for breath.

No one remembered the soldier who had collapsed after being bitten until someone spotted his drowned corpse floating face-down in the water, swarming with dark, hairy shapes.

Most of the bitten men were helped along by their comrades, suffering from varying degrees of muscle cramps, irregular heartbeats or shortness of breath. A few became delirious and a few others simply passed out. These men had to be carried, a nearly impossible task in the deep mud. The column pressed forward, each man passing the word back to avoid the area, and the line curved in a wide bow into the swamp before coming back in, further slowing the advance. Nagazawa was half dragged, half carried for nearly an hour before he regained some of his strength and could walk on his own.

Shoji and Sgt. Shimizu checked their platoon. Two had been bitten, but were limping along supported by their friends, gasping for breath but still coherent. The lieutenant shuddered, reliving the feel of the vile creature scampering across his face. He had been wishing the colonel would call a break, thinking that he might take a chance and spend a few minutes leaning against a mangrove to rest his back and legs. Now the thought gave him a chill. He wasn't going near a mangrove.

It was three in the morning when the British guns roared again, a brief series of three salvos from the battleship, and this time their guesswork paid off. 381mm shells rained down on the column, blowing apart mangrove trees and soldiers alike in a barrage which lasted only twelve minutes but felt like hours. There was nowhere to run, not that running was even possible, and men found themselves mired in place as the big rounds burst in plumes of water and fragmented wood and whizzing metal. Limbs were sheared off in a blink, chests were torn apart, entire bodies disappeared from being too close to a hit, and above the blasts were the screams. Most men dropped below the surface, holding their breath, hoping to escape the blasts, but the fast-moving shrapnel cut through water as easily as flesh.

And then it was over, the night dropping back into place, filled with the groans and wails of the wounded. Shoji rose from where he was crouched with only his nose and eyes above the surface, and ran his hands over his body, looking for wounds. He was untouched. Others were not so lucky.

It took the officers an hour to pull the regiment back into a column and assess the damage. Twenty-seven killed, thirty-one wounded, and sixteen of those so severely they would not live without serious medical attention. Five of the dead and three of the wounded came from Shoji Kichida's platoon. Riku, the gunner's assistant had lost his right arm at the elbow and was sagging in the arms of the big Dai, who wept and held the boy like a child. A tourniquet was all that kept Riku from bleeding to death.

Sergeant Shimizu had been decapitated.

Colonel Nagazawa assembled his officers and listened to the casualty reports, his face an expressionless mask. Shoji looked at each man as they spoke, and was happy to see Tatsuya among them, his round face lumpy with insect bites but alive nonetheless. Tatsuya gave Shoji a wink and a grin.

The colonel considered the numbers for a moment and then nodded. "We are moving out. The wounded who can walk on their own will accompany the column. Those who cannot must be left behind."

Shocked silence greeted the order.

"It is our duty to deliver as large a force as possible to the mainland. The wounded will only delay us further."

A very young captain cleared his throat. "Colonel, our men will die if left here unattended."

"Yes," said Nagazawa. "They will make a glorious sacrifice for the Emperor by not interfering with our advance. Heroes all." He turned his head to look at his other officers, the big spider bite on his neck making him wince with the motion. "Sort the wounded. We move in ten minutes."

"Sir, their suffering…we…we cannot…" The captain's eyes were pleading.

"Put them out of their misery then, Captain." Nagazawa's falcon eyes were hard. The younger officer's mouth simply hung open. He wasn't about to shoot his own wounded men, nor would he issue such an order. His soldiers would refuse in any event.

As the officers started to drift away, the captain turned to a subordinate and instructed him to begin collecting canteens to leave with the wounded men. Nagazawa snapped at him. "You will do no such thing! This regiment will need all its provisions to complete this march, especially water. You will leave them nothing."

"Colonel!" the man shouted, his face turning red.

Nagazawa's right hand dropped to his sidearm and he locked eyes. "You have something more to say?"

The captain trembled, his hands clenched into fists, and then he was like a balloon which has had all the air let out of it. He hung his head and moved away without a word. The other officers did the same.

It was a decision which did not sit well with the men, and there were many arguments, protests about the order being dishonorable, that carrying the wounded would create no additional burden, that with the column was moving as slowly as it was, the men could easily keep up. NCOs and officers gave terse commands, not wanting to discuss it, knowing they had no words to justify it, stating only that the colonel was to be obeyed. A few men had to be threatened with execution before they relented.

Private Sasaki sneered at Riku's missing arm. "He's dead weight anyway."

Dai blinked at him, then gently handed Riku to another soldier. When he turned back he punched Sasaki in the face so hard that men five feet away heard bones crunch. Sasaki went down, and Dai advanced on him. His face was impassive, but his eyes held murder. It took three men to drag him away.

The malingerer pulled himself out of the water, holding his face in both hands and standing unsteadily, blood streaming through his fingers and dripping into the swamp. He did not approach the gunner, who stood with fists clenched, waiting. Instead he looked at his lieutenant, who had seen the whole thing.

"Well, what are you going to do about that?" His voice was thick and nasally.

Shoji looked back at him. "Nothing. But I am going to wonder what Dai will do to you once I walk away." Then he did just that, half-expecting to hear a snarl and the breaking of bones, but it didn't come. Perhaps Dai had simply drowned him quietly. Shoji didn't really care.

As Nagazawa ordered, the wounded who could not keep up were gathered around a trio of mangroves. Someone strung rope between the trees and lashed a few empty wooden ammo crates to it in an attempt to give them something to sit on or lean against. One man, unconscious and bleeding from a head wound, was tied to a tree to prevent him from sliding under the surface. More than a few soldiers thought he looked like a meal trussed up and awaiting whatever lived up in those branches.

Dai carried Riku in his powerful arms and set him down carefully next to a red mangrove, inspecting the trunk before leaning the boy against it. "I have to go, now."

Riku clutched at his uniform with his remaining hand. "Please don't leave me here."

"I have to go." Dai choked on the words.

Riku started crying. "Kill me, Dai. Please kill me. Don't leave me like this."

The big gunner wiped at his eyes, his chest heaving, then pulled a grenade off his belt and pressed it into the boy's hand. "Strike the arming pin against the tree," he whispered. "Then hold it under your chin." He pressed his forehead against the boy's for a long moment, then turned and waded back to the column. Riku watched him go, clutching the grenade.

Shoji looked on from nearby, fighting to keep from choking out a sob of his own. Dai passed him without a word, his cheeks wet with tears, and Shoji looked down in shame. In the moonlight he watched the blood of the wounded pool on top of the swamp water like a black oil slick, slowly drifting away from the gathering of men.

Blood in the water, he thought. Our enemies scent it like predators, and they won't stop until they make the kill. He stared long at the collection of wounded men, then turned and followed Dai.

Ten minutes later they heard the muffled blast of a grenade going off behind them.

Colonel Nagazawa forced them to march for another three hours, until the sky grew light. By that point the regiment had traveled a total of four miles, barely a third of the distance. In the grayness above, the sun was not even risen, but already the temperature was soaring past one hundred degrees, the humidity oppressive and causing a thick haze to settle over the swamp. In the early hours the tide had gone out, leaving only a three inch film of water.

Up on point, Lieutenant Masato reported back that he had come to a place with a large clearing, a space in the swamp empty of trees, approximately fifty yards wide and a hundred yards across. The colonel was moving forward to see this for himself, and to decide how best to move the column, most likely through the trees around one edge or the other. Within thirty minutes he sent back the order that the regiment would hold position for three hours and that the men could sleep, provided sentries were posted.

Soldiers collapsed into the mud at once, dropping their weapons into the brine. They propped their heads on helmets or packs to keep their faces out of the water, and fell asleep immediately. Shoji longed to join them, but first he selected four men – Sasaki among them – and ordered a pair to stand an hour and a half watch before the second pair relieved them. Sasaki glared with unconcealed hatred for his officer, his nose a mashed, red lump under blackened eyes, but said nothing.

Minutes later, Shoji dropped as well and rested his head on his pack, quickly slipping into a doze. His body settled slowly into the soft mud, and it conformed to his shape, cradling him. He didn't notice the stench, didn't feet the sharp poke of oysters, didn't feel the rising heat or notice the black flies emerging from holes in the mud in places where it rose above the water, crawling over faces and mud-caked uniforms. He was already dreaming, and in his dreams he was flying, coasting low over white crested waves, the brown pelican soaring beside him, brushing his fingertips with its wings. Perhaps he would turn north, and fly back to Satcheko. Would she still love him if he was a bird? Shoji smiled in his sleep.

Private Sasaki watched the men fall still, hating them for their ability to sleep when he could not, staring at Dai's snoring form and hating him more. Despising the lieutenant most of all. He fantasized about snapping his bayonet onto the end of his rifle and driving it through that snot-nosed Kichida's throat, then serving up the same fate to the machine-gunner. He imagined how they would choke and gurgle on their own blood, looking up at him with surprise, begging for help, and how he would laugh at them.

But Sasaki would do none of those things. He was a coward and he knew it. Instead, once he was certain they were all asleep and the other sentry was looking the other way, he plodded among the men closest to him, gathering the few canteens he could find still holding water and stuffing them into his pack. Surrendering to the British might mean torture followed by execution, as the Colonel often warned, but he had also heard rumors that prisoners were treated decently, given food and water and even medical attention. It was worth the risk. Anyplace was better than here.

With a last look back to confirm he wasn't being watched, he slipped away into the mangroves.

8

The three hours of promised rest ended at an hour and a half. A lone spotter plane buzzed low over the swamp several times, and then went away. Half an hour later the bombers arrived. Shoji and the men of the 121st were shocked awake by the blast of two-hundred pound bombs tearing the mangroves apart, sending up clouds of mud and shattered wood, shrapnel singing through the air. Men hugged the mud or scrambled for cover behind trees, orders were shouted and unheard over the explosions, though the screams somehow pierced through. It was over in minutes.

Shoji untucked from his fetal position against the base of a red mangrove and looked around. A few trees had been cut in half, blossoms of pale wood splinters jutting from stumps like sharp flowers. Some of the men were getting to their feet, but others were still, face down in the brine, red spreading out from their motionless forms.

The lieutenant saw Yoichi and Dai emerging from behind a tangle of brush, and waved them over.

"You're both corporals now," he said. "Assemble the platoon and get them moving forward. I don't care if the platoon in front of us is moving yet or not, we are. And try to get me a headcount and the names of our casualties."

The men nodded and trudged away through the mud.

Shoji took off his cap and wiped at his brow, succeeding only in smearing it with mud. How long before the naval guns started? Would the spotter plane return to check on the bombers' work, see how accurate they had been? There was no way the enemy would fail to notice the regiment moving in daylight. He yawned, his body aching everywhere at once, the brief sleep more of a tease than rest with any value. But it was all they were going to get. And the first shift sentries would see no rest at all. He knew he'd hear about that from Sasaki.

He realized he had been standing in one place, staring at nothing for some time, his brain in a waking doze, and he shook his head. In front of him was a man-sized plant growing in the salty mud, its broad leaf encrusted with salt crystals. How could it live like that? He stared at the crystals, at the intricate pattern of dark green veins, at the scalloped edges of the leaves. Shoji blinked his eyes. He was doing it again, fatigue robbing him of his senses. Around him men were forming up the column and moving. Shoji pulled a canteen from his pack – he only had two left which were full – and sipped, then carefully poured some into his palm and rubbed it into his eyes. It seemed to help.

As the lieutenant plodded towards the front of his platoon, Yoichi and Dai reported in. The bombing had killed three, wounded two others, but they were well enough to move. Sasaki was missing.

"Is he lying wounded somewhere? Could you have missed him?"

They shook their heads.

Shoji cursed softly and went to find the colonel to deliver the casualty report.

The expected naval bombardment didn't come, and the bombers didn't return. Single engine spotter planes floated above in the gray sky from time to time, but appeared unable to locate the column. As the morning stretched out, it seemed the enemy had lost interest in killing them.

The swamp had other ideas.

Colonel Nagazawa ordered the regiment to curve left around the open area Lt. Masato had found, instructing that the men stay at least twenty feet inside the tree line as they moved. The clearing had been transformed into a gray mudflat with a scattering of rotting stumps and pools of deeper standing water. Black flies and mosquitoes swarmed in clouds over the flats, and a few small, quick lizards scampered over the surface to dine on them. The stench of the mud was overpowering, and the soldiers tied rags or shirts over their faces to keep it out.

The sticky haze hung on throughout the morning, the rising heat and humidity quickly draining the remaining canteens. Men sagged in their packs, heads bobbed on chests and arms dangled. Soldiers passed out and crashed to the mud, their friends trying to revive them by splashing the murky brine into their faces. They stripped off uniform shirts and marched on bare chested, their exposed flesh an invitation to mosquitoes and biting flies that fed without interference from men too tired to wave them away.

The troops of the 121st had been skinny to begin with, weeks without resupply and quarter rations supplemented with maggoty rice conspiring to draw skin tight against ribs and jawbones. Now, as they sweated under the grueling heat, unable to replace the fluids leaving their bodies, they grew even more drawn. Soon they would appear as skeletons with packs and helmets and rifles.

They marched in silence, mud spilling over the tops of their boots and adding weight, making each step agony. Despite the absence of the hip deep water, which should have allowed them to move faster, the regiment was slowing down.

Shoji walked beside two privates at the head of his platoon, boys who had only recently arrived on Ramree. At first he strained to remember their names, but soon gave up. His uniform shirt, which he refused to remove since he was an officer and was required to maintain a minimum of decorum despite the environment, was soaked and dark, salt crystals clinging to seams and creases, rubbing at his neck. He had handed his remaining rations and other full canteen to the men, but still his pack dragged at his shoulders as if it contained river stones. His lungs pulled at the damp air, making him wheeze, the salt drying his lips and turning them white. Shoji's boots lifted and fell on their own now as he climbed over exposed roots and fought against the pulling mud, unsure if his grayed vision was a result of the haze or an indication he was about to pass out.

The flies and mosquitoes were unrelenting, and the biting ants were back, only without water in which a soldier could submerge to drown them. At midday there was a shriek just ahead of him, followed by a whining babble and the shouts of alarmed men. Shoji slogged forward, meeting the other platoon's officer at a point where several men were crouched around a fallen soldier. The man in the mud was convulsing and foaming, his eyes rolled back in his head, his right elbow a swelling, purple and black mass which quickly made his entire arm balloon.

Shoji stared in horror, then looked up to where the excited soldiers were pointing. He caught a glimpse of a centipede twisting its way up the curved trunk of a mangrove, moving swiftly into the canopy. It was covered in white and bright purple bands, and was as long and thick as his forearm.

The soldier on the ground convulsed hard enough that Shoji thought his spine might crack, his face swelling and turning that evil, purple-black, and then he was still, foam trickling from the corner of his mouth. A small crab trundled across the mud towards the corpse, instinctively drawn to a meal. Shoji crushed it under his boot and went back to his platoon.

Of the fifty soldiers Lt. Kichida commanded as the regiment stepped off yesterday, only twenty-nine remained. Few were veterans, and most were just boys collected from their farms and villages and thrown into service with minimal training. He was almost certain one of the boys in his mortar squad was fifteen. If that. Those still with him were exhausted, and many were sick.

How many would he deliver into Burma? Any? Would he make it himself? Violent death was a certainty he had forced himself to acknowledge once he entered the infantry, at least on an intellectual level. It was part of *Bushido*, a fatalistic reality embraced by the samurai of old, idealism expected of modern day Japanese military officers. That acceptance of death supposedly removed all fear, making them more dangerous in combat. But Shoji knew he was not samurai. For him, fear of death had been driven from him like a peasant whipping his oxen, the endless brutality of war accompanied by fatigue and deprivation making him simply not care anymore. But dying in this unclean place was offensive, an end unworthy of soldiers. It was something he would not wish even upon those who were trying to kill him, and a fate from which he desperately wanted to spare his men. No one deserved to die here. Shoji decided that whether he survived or not, he would see as many of his troops as he could safely across.

And where was that noble love for your men when you ordered the wounded left behind? When you condemned men loyal to you and the Empire to a prolonged and painful death at the hands of this merciless place? The unpleasant voice had returned. *How dare you pretend to care about them, when you know you would walk across each of their bodies in order to save yourself?*

Shoji didn't bother to tell the voice to shut up. It didn't listen anyway.

He checked on Matsuda and learned that the boy's malaria was advancing. He was jaundiced and vomiting, and his retinas were turning white. Shoji knew that rigor and convulsions would soon follow.

"He can still keep up," said newly-promoted Corporal Yoichi. "I'll look after him."

Shoji looked at him. "And when you fall behind and can no longer look after him? You know the colonel's orders."

"I'm not leaving him to be eaten alive by this fucking swamp." Yoichi's voice was steady, not challenging, simply stating a fact.

Shoji looked at the sick boy, only on his feet because another soldier was holding him up. The lieutenant said nothing, just nodded and squeezed Yoichi's shoulder before moving on. That was when the first cramp hit him, a clenched fist twisting deep in his guts, doubling him over. He felt his bowels let go, loose and runny, sliding down his legs. Bent over and unable to stand, his face burning with shame, he saw stringers of bloody mucus dripping from the torn cuffs of his trousers where they had come loose from their leggings. I'm shitting blood, he thought, as another cramp bent his insides in the other direction. Shoji cried out.

Big hands took him firmly by the shoulders and forced him to slowly straighten. “Not even the Emperor deserves a bow that deep,” Dai whispered, holding his officer close to make sure he didn’t fall. He gave Shoji’s shoulders a reassuring squeeze. “No one noticed, Lieutenant.”

Shoji’s cheeks burned.

“It’s dysentery, everyone has it. There are men who are worse off, starting to get delirious.”

Shoji shook his head, realizing this was a stupid place to be embarrassed about crapping himself. Nobody cared, and the stink of the mud was far worse. He thanked the big gunner, who nodded and returned to the column. Shoji stood for a moment, looking at the thin trails of blood running from his boots across the mud, dissipating in the brine. Blood in the water.

He returned to the march.

9

The colonel called a fifteen minute break around noon. The men barely had time to drop to the mud before the Phoebe's and Queen Elizabeth's guns began rolling, the air filled with the high-pitched shrieks of heavy shells dropping in lines across the swamp. The opening salvo was well forward and to the left of the regiment, the blasts muffled, clouds of smoke seen rising over the treetops. But then another salvo came in, this one closer. The men scattered and found what cover they could, mostly among the sprawling roots of the mangroves.

And as the shells marched nearer with each passing minute, making the ground tremble, the men of the 121st discovered that the trees among which they sought shelter also sheltered something else. Hundreds of large, black scorpions.

The creatures were fast and aggressive, racing down trunks and scuttling out from the darkness of root clusters, running over the mud, tails held high. Unconcerned with the shaking earth or trees, they were on the huddling men in moments, stinging backs and arms and necks and faces, able to sting again and again, pincers locking onto fingers and earlobes.

Soldiers screamed and slapped at them, knocking them away only to have them flip over and race back in. Some men stomped them into the mud, but those with bare feet succeeded only in being stung on their soles and ankles. The branches overhead rustled with crawling life as more ran down to join the attack.

Shoji jerked off his helmet and used it to bat them away, to crush others against the trees, but they were hard-shelled and quick, dodging sideways or simply recovering from the blow. He saw a man in front of him using a bayonet to stab at them, saw him strike at a scorpion running up his leg, missing and burying the blade in his thigh. Another man's face was covered with them, and he shrieked hysterically, ripping them off, his face welting and one eye already swollen shut.

Naval artillery rounds screamed overhead and began hitting the regiment to Shoji's rear, red flashes and deafening concussions blooming through the trees, the shapes of torn bodies pin-wheeling through the air. Men overcome with fear and revulsion at the scorpions stood to try to shake them off, and were cut down by shrapnel. Others knelt in the mud and used their rifle butts to crush the creatures and struck out at their friends, killing scorpions which had crawled up their backs. Everyone was screaming.

A whistle blew up ahead, and Shoji struggled to his feet and began waving his arms. "Forward! Start moving forward!" He hauled slapping and crying men to their feet and pushed them along. "We have to get away from them!" He crushed a running scorpion under a boot heel.

The soldiers responded and stumbled after one another, watching the ground and the trees, stomping and swinging rifles, using their helmets to bat them off one another. As with the spiders, word was sent back to swing around the area, though Shoji couldn't help but wonder what new horror would await those troops. The column was on its feet and moving, the moans and cries for help from the severely wounded ignored. One man with his legs blown off at the knees was lying in the mud, reaching a hand towards the departing men as black scorpions swarmed over his back, stinging repeatedly. The soldiers looked away and tried to move faster.

Shoji checked behind, saw that the company following was well back and disorganized, but he had his own men to worry about, and kept them together. As they moved, he could still see scorpions in the trees and on the ground, but not nearly as many as before. They must have blundered into a large nest of some sort. He doubted they had seen the last of them, and indeed men continued to crush the creatures when they ventured too close, wary of low-hanging branches and the ominous dark spaces among large root clusters.

Corporals Yoichi and Dai found him and reported four more men lost, not specifying whether it had been due to the shelling or the scorpions. Several minutes later a runner came down the line, summoning officers for a meeting with Nagazawa.

The colonel looked like a boxer who had come up on the losing end of a match with a particularly brutal opponent. His face was misshapen by welts and bites, and one ear had been partially severed by shrapnel. The regiment's only surviving medic stood beside him, trying to hold a gauze pad to the side of the man's head. The officers gave him their casualty reports and water status – there was none - and Nagazawa responded that by nightfall they should be at the half way point. There would be no more rest until he called a halt at sunset. He also said that despite the enemy bombing and naval artillery, the regiment remained a force of seven-hundred fifty men, a number he considered acceptable.

Two of the officers hesitated before reporting they had desertions, handfuls of men who slipped away during the brief rest period. Shoji stayed quiet, not mentioning Private Sasaki.

“How do you know they deserted?” Nagazawa asked softly.

One lieutenant stated his sergeant had heard several men talking about it earlier, and now that they were missing that was his assumption. The other young officer announced that he had seen his deserters running off with his own eyes.

The colonel stared at him. “And why did you not shoot them, Lieutenant?”

The man looked down. “I tried, sir, but my sidearm would not fire. The mud.”

“Was I unclear when I ordered you all to keep discipline within your ranks?”

Shaking heads.

“Which would include properly working weapons. If we have no means to fight, what will we do if the enemy lands troops in this swamp?”

Let them have it, Shoji thought, and saw Tatsuya across the circle of officers. His friend seemed to know his thoughts and gave him a smirk and a wink.

Nagazawa looked around at his subordinates. "You will set the example for your troops. You will ensure your weapons are properly cleaned, and enforce the same with the men." His eyes narrowed. "Anyone seen discarding weapons or ammunition in order to lighten their load will be shot. By you. Is that clear?"

"Hai!" they responded as a group.

"Lt. Kami," the colonel said, pointing at the officer who had been unable to stop his deserting men. "You are demoted to rifleman. Report to Lt. Masato and instruct him you are to be assigned to the point." The man gave a slow, deflated bow. "But first find your platoon sergeant and tell him he is promoted to lieutenant and platoon leader." He glared at them all, then ordered them back to their units.

Tatsuya walked with Shoji for a bit.

"That could have been me," Shoji said. "My pistol is fouled by this damned mud, and even if it wasn't I need a complete stripping to clear the salt. There is no chance it would fire."

“Mine is the same. So is everyone’s. Many of the men don’t even have their weapons anymore. Are we supposed to shoot them because they have nothing to clean?”

They walked without speaking for a time.

“Are you bitten much?” Tatsuya asked finally. It was an attempt at humor. Both men were covered in bite marks and welts

“Take your pick by what creature.”

“I heard about the centipede, heard you saw it. Was it really that large?” He held his hands apart as if demonstrating the size of a fish which had escaped the hook. Shoji took his hands and moved them several more inches apart. The man stared at the length, then shoved his hands in his pockets.

“The scorpion bites burn for a bit and leave the flesh sore, but so far no other effects. Not as bad as the tarantulas.”

“I’ve missed both,” said Tatsuya. “We’re far enough back that we got the word before we walked into it.”

“Lucky,” said Shoji.

Tatsuya shrugged. "Lucky is a very subjective word. We caught direct hits from the last bombardment. I'm down to nineteen men."

Shoji looked at him wide-eyed. "You marched in with nearly forty!"

His friend gave him a lopsided grin. "Ah, now you're talking about lucky. Like I said before, we still have to be here. If this keeps up, soon I'll be just a squad leader."

Shoji wished he could share Tatsuya's casual attitude about losing men – if it truly was that, and not merely bravado – and found that the more he lost, the more fiercely he wanted to save the ones remaining. And yes, he told the nasty voice, that includes me.

"We owe it to ourselves to get piss drunk when this is over," Tatsuya announced.

"And we will," Shoji said, telling himself there actually would be an *after*, and not believing it.

His friend shot him another grin, then turned away to meet up with his dwindling platoon. The next time Shoji saw him, Tatsuya would be screaming and begging for death.

10

Private Sasaki was lost. Everywhere he moved, everywhere he looked appeared the same, twisted red and black mangrove trees rising out of the mud and thin water, exposed roots arching in every direction seeking nutrients. Huge green leaves sprouted from pale stalks, crawling with ants, forcing him to double back and find another way through in order to avoid them. The mud threatened to bring him to a complete stop, loose and wet on the surface, but tight once his bare feet sank into it. Overhead an intense, washed-out light pressed down through the canopy, the sun nowhere in sight and useless for navigation. All he wanted was the edge of the swamp, to find the ocean, but it eluded him.

Haze hugged the ground, dense in some places, thin in others, but heavy as a wool coat dipped in a water barrel. The heat made his vision swim, and he had exhausted the last of his stolen canteens hours ago. He didn't know what time it was, how long he had been moving – it seemed like forever - didn't know if he was turning in a circle which would lead him back to the regiment and a swift execution for desertion. He hoped it would be swift. That bastard Kichida would probably tie him to a tree, bayonet him in the guts and leave him there to die slowly.

Sasaki was stripped to the waist, and he had cut his trousers away at mid-thigh with his bayonet, which he carried in one hand. His helmet, pack and rifle had been discarded some time ago. Thirst raged in him, the heat sucking moisture from his body, and at one point he could resist no longer and dropped to his knees, cupping the muddy brown water film atop the mud into his hands and drinking. He gagged, choking on the salt water, his throat burning. Sasaki began to weep, instantly wishing he hadn't done it.

The private staggered to his feet and pushed on, holding onto trees for support, no longer avoiding the plants swarming with ants, letting them bite him as he blundered forward. The swamp was endless, an unchanging maze which would suck him under, filling his lungs with drowning mud so that ants and spiders could feed upon his remains. Without realizing it, he began to let out a constant groaning, and his face pulled taut in a monstrous grin.

From up ahead came a whisper, then silence, then a whisper again. The sound repeated itself over and over. Sasaki decided it was Death calling his name in a language only it understood, summoning him. He grinned wider, tripping over a root and then righting himself, moving towards the whispering. He didn't feel the sting on the back of his left hand, didn't see the scorpion on the tree trunk, or the half dozen others running across the branches around him. It was getting brighter, Death showing him the way with a steadily brightening light which made his whitened retinas burn. Malaria coursed through his body – he actually hadn't been lying when he said he was sick – sapping his strength, making his muscles rigid, his fever climbing with each passing hour. He doggedly moved towards the brightness as water began washing over his shins, then his knees, the whisper turning into a great shushing sound.

Private Sasaki stopped and blinked, cool water surging against his legs, then rushing back out a moment later. He held up an arm to shield his eyes from the light, wincing and trying to see. Where was Death? He was ready, so ready to put this horror behind him.

He was at the shore, the ocean spreading out before him in greens and blues, waves sloshing against him. Death was waiting for him just offshore, a dark shape atop the water, the details of the figure clouded by his fever and delirium. He sobbed and fell to his knees, water surging against his sun-burned and bitten chest. Sasaki raised his arms over his head and waved at Death, trying to speak, trying to scream.

"I've found you! Take me now! Take me away!"

Private Fairweather caught movement to the right and snapped up his binoculars. An emaciated man was kneeling in the surf forty yards away, waving his arms.

He shouted before he realized it. "Target, two o'clock!"

In front of him, Specialist Browne spun his turret to the right, and then his .50 caliber rattled, casings tinkling on the deck. The man on shore fell in a red puff, and Browne's machinegun fell silent.

"Any more?" barked Sgt. Bremer.

Fairweather's heart was hammering as he tracked his binoculars back and forth across the tree line. After a moment he yelled, "No, Sergeant!"

Bremer leaned over the armored shield and patted the young man on the helmet. "We'll make a marine of you yet, Fairweather."

The private grinned, but it quickly faded. He stopped looking for Japs in the trees, thinking only of the skinny, waving man cut down in a burst of red. He swallowed hard. He was going to be sick again.

11

The afternoon was endless. Temperatures reached a staggering high of one-hundred-thirteen, causing heat stroke and in one case death. Biting flies, ants and swarms of mosquitoes feasted on the men, and the scorpions attacked whenever the men came near them. As it turned out, Shoji was wrong in his analysis of their toxins being nothing more than an inconvenience. The venom took a couple hours to take effect, resulting in painful paralysis. Those stung in the neck or face died.

Thirst swept through the ranks, further shortening tempers and bringing on delirium, men getting sick as they tried to drink the fetid swamp water, despite orders to the contrary. The malaria cases got worse, the dysentery – Shoji's included – grew increasingly painful, and as the day stretched out, the tides returned, the water deepening steadily and slowing the column.

The British had apparently decided the fleeing Japanese were still worth killing, and attacked sporadically from the sea and air, their shells and bombs often missing, but occasionally finding their marks. Per orders, the maimed and disabled were left behind, gathered together by soldiers with blank expressions and glassy eyes. By now there were no words of comfort offered, and no water to be left behind.

As the regiment continued forward it left a blood trail, a trail which had not gone unnoticed. They were being followed, and not by British marines. Unknown to the men of the 121st, not a single wounded man they left behind remained alive. Most died screaming.

Colonel Nagazawa called a halt at sunset, and as with the night before, there was no place for the men to sit down without drowning, and they had learned by now to stay away from the trees. Scorpions by day, tarantulas by night. There was no word on how long the rest period would last. A few enterprising soldiers managed to use their shirts to net handfuls of small fish, and soon the entire regiment was turned into fishermen. They were salty – probably a bad idea, some thought – but provided a burst of liquid as they were chewed, and put at least something into shrinking bellies.

Cpl. Dai managed to find a submerged mangrove stump just beneath the water's surface, and guided his lieutenant to it, insisting he sit. Shoji protested, but Dai told him rank had its privileges, and a few minutes later returned with a fistful of the tiny, salty fish. Shoji thanked him, told him he would sit for only five minutes, and that he wanted Dai to rotate every man in the platoon for a ten minute rest on the stump, starting with the corporal.

He eyed the fish, knowing they would only make him thirstier than he already was, but in the end he gobbled down every one, savoring the taste and the act of chewing and swallowing. No meal ever prepared in his mother's kitchen came close to matching this feast. He still had half a canteen in his pack, carefully guarded all through the march, but resisted the urge to drink. At the speed they were going, they would not be leaving this place any time soon, and he would be thankful he had it later.

As he sat with his hips submerged, he let his muscles relax and risked closing his eyes. He tried to picture Satcheko standing in front of his parent's house, slender and beautiful in her kimono, snow falling lightly around her and landing softly on her black hair. He couldn't make the image appear. All he could summon was a scorched crater in the earth with shattered bones at the bottom.

His thoughts returned to the swamp. He never could have imagined a place on earth as vile as this, could not have conceived of the horrors that lived here, or the way sun and heat and water could combine so efficiently to extinguish a man's life. Everything which existed here was trying to kill them, a perfect formula of death. A garden of torment.

Before this the most frightening thing Shoji could imagine was a tiger. The jungles of Burma were filled with them, and during his time there, before his assignment to Ramree, his greatest fear was not the enemy, but of pushing through thick undergrowth and stumbling upon one of those big cats. He had nightmares of being torn apart by jaws and powerful claws, of being dragged off and eaten.

There had been a tiger on Ramree once, a big male which the locals spoke of with fearful respect, a solitary killer prowling the tall grasses and shadowy jungle, lord of its small world. By the time he reported for duty on Ramree, however, the tiger had been killed and turned into a rug on Colonel Nagazawa's office floor. He doubted the colonel had hunted and killed the beast himself.

They had all been taught that soldiers of Japan were supposed to be tigers too, powerful killers dominating and destroying weaker, inferior life. Ferocious and unstoppable. But it was all a lie. Shoji knew that a real tiger, especially the Ramree tiger, was too smart to enter this place of death. It would prefer to go out fighting, proud and strong, rather than live out its final days in helpless, perpetual pain, dying a foot at a time.

He was dozing now, and about to fall off the stump when he was awakened by a voice nearby saying the word, "Yellow." He opened his eyes, and in the twilight saw Private Yamada, the locomotive fireman, standing fifteen feet away beside another man and pointing to something on a mangrove trunk. Shoji saw the object of their interest, a hairy caterpillar the size of a man's thumb, so bright yellow it appeared to glow in the falling light.

Then the caterpillar exploded.

It didn't really explode, but to Shoji that was how it appeared as a puff of inch-long, yellow hairs burst from the insect in a little cloud. In the language of the Ramree natives it was called *Buung Haan,* translated loosely as 'Yellow Madness.' The locals knew well enough to keep away from it, and hadn't bothered to warn their invaders of its dangers. Matsuda and his friend laughed at being startled and watched the caterpillar crawl up the tree, while the small cloud of hairs floated downward, coming to rest on their bare arms, chests and necks.

The chemical reaction was instantaneous.

The two men let out a piercing scream and began clawing at their skin, slapping and wailing. Matsuda's friend, eyes wide, began biting at his own arms, ripping at the flesh, falling into the water and erupting a moment later with a new shriek. His nails left red furrows across his chest, and he hurled himself against a mangrove, slamming his head and face repeatedly against the wood.

Matsuda screeched like an owl and began clawing his own eyes out, babbling and whipping his head from side to side.

Soldiers splashed towards them, fearful and looking all around, checking the darkening canopy. Had the spiders returned? The scorpions? Shoji pushed through them to see that the second soldier was now leaving a bloody imprint on the tree where he was banging his head, still digging at his skin and gibbering. A man tried to pull him away but the soldier turned on him and began hammering with his fists, bloody spittle flying from a mouth full of broken teeth.

Matsuda was blind, both eyes gone and now clawing at his ears, trying to rip them off, his face a bloody mask as he continued to screech. Shoji looked from one man to the other, his heart slamming in his chest, and then he pulled his pistol from its flap holster. It was now thoroughly cleaned, as he had been instructed. He raised his arm as the soldiers of his platoon leapt to get out of the way, then fired a single round into the man's head. The body dropped into the water and out of sight as if a trap door had been opened beneath it.

He turned to Matsuda, still standing in one place, his body twitching uncontrollably and his head still thrashing, one ear nearly off now and his animal screaming carrying far through the swamp. Shoji held his breath, aimed, and shot him in the forehead. He fell like his companion, and then there was a sudden vacuum of silence. No one moved, no one spoke. Shoji stared at the bloody water for a full minute, then holstered his pistol and waded away.

Tigers of the Empire, brought down by a caterpillar.

12

It began just as night was coming on, the heat of the day slipping down into the nineties, beams of moonlight shining down through the leaves and branches overhead. The regiment was slowly moving again, exhausted men plodding through the hip deep water in a long, snaking line.

Corporal Yoichi had been spared his promise that he would see the malaria-afflicted Matsuda safely through. The seventeen-year-old fisherman died vomiting and convulsing just before the order came to step off. Yoichi held him through it all, and then gently let the boy slip under the water's surface.

Shoji's platoon was now positioned fourth back from the head of the column. Everyone had heard the sporadic bursts of heavy machinegun fire off to their right in the late afternoon, removing any doubt that the enemy was still out there, still committed to seeing the 121st never left Ramree. Some speculated that the firing was nothing more than random probes designed to give the retreating soldiers no rest. Colonel Nagazawa used it to confirm his statement that the British were preparing to land troops, and that the soldiers of the 121st would soon find themselves in contact with the enemy. His words had little effect on the dead-tired, thirsty men, many of whom preferred the thought of a bullet to this torture which existed somewhere outside of time.

The screaming came from the front, coming through the darkness in a wild burst cut suddenly short. A moment later there was another scream from the same direction, the hollow crack of a pistol, more screaming. The men in the column instinctively spread out to the right and left, taking cover behind trees. Those who hadn't cleaned their weapons as instructed cursed themselves and tried desperately to wipe away the worst of the mud and salt. Eyes struggled to see in the gloom.

A long silence followed, and then the platoons were reforming and moving forward. Shoji got his men together quickly, as curious as the rest of them. It took a half hour before his part of the column came to a point where the colonel and several officers were gathered, one using an uncovered flashlight to pan through the trees. Apparently the order for light discipline no longer mattered. Nagazawa was holding a helmet.

"What happened?"

The colonel frowned. "British commandos. They ambushed our men on the point, dragged the bodies away."

The point. That included Lt. Kami, the one who had disgraced himself and been demoted. "Commandos?" Shoji asked without thinking, looking around at the dark swamp. "I heard screaming."

Nagazawa made a sour face. "Yes, commandos, as I have been warning all along. Get back to your units and keep your men sharp." He stomped through the water and tossed the helmet aside. It floated upside-down, turning slowly. In the moonlight Shoji could see the interior was slick with blood, and the steel had a long gouge in it. A commando would ambush by stealth, with a knife. There would have been no screaming.

Shoji watched his commander disappear into the darkness, then rejoined his men.

Fifteen minutes later there was another scream from the front, a long wailing that seemed to bounce off the trees. Then another, much closer, a commotion of excited and fearful voices. Shoji was beside Cpl. Yoichi and ordered him to have the men spread out, unholstering his pistol as a chorus of cries came from the platoon behind him, followed by a pair of quick rifle shots. He strained to see, angry again that he had lost his glasses, but knowing they wouldn't have helped much in the darkness. A deep, ugly croaking came from the shadows behind him, answered by similar sounds on the column's left flank, then rebounding back to the right again.

Sporadic cracks of rifles ahead and behind, voices calling frantically in the night. Shoji moved next to a young soldier aiming his rifle into the darkness, his weapon shaking as he tracked the barrel back and forth.

"Know what you are shooting at before you fire," Shoji said.

The boy nodded, and then a mass of darkness exploded from the water in front of him, a wide head twisting sideways and huge jaws snapping together on the boy's midsection. He shrieked and squeezed the trigger, the flash from the rifle giving an instant's glimpse of ridges and black scales and huge yellow eyes. In a second the boy was pulled under, the water boiling like an uncovered pot, the black mass rolling and thrashing, tearing the body apart.

Blood and water splashed across Shoji's face, and he cried out, firing three, four, five shots at the giant shape, which quickly submerged. He didn't know if he hit it, didn't have time to wonder, for in that moment his platoon was hit from both sides. Nightmares erupted from the water, pulling men under in seconds, guttural snarls and roars filling the air in a ghastly duet with screaming men. A few rifles went off, not many, and then to the rear of Shoji's platoon there was the dull *CRUMP* of a grenade exploding.

Heavy splashing now in the darkness on both sides, more deep croaking. Men stood back to back facing outwards, those with jammed weapons quickly snapping on bayonets. Shoji yelled for them to move in close together, to form rings. He found Dai and put his back to the gunner, who had his weapon supported by a sling and leveled at the water, one hand cradling a belt of ammunition, ready to fire.

Wounded soldiers sobbed in the night, others cried out for medics who didn't exist and still more shouted back and forth, firing into the night. Shoji heard a man babbling for his mother well out in the darkness, still alive as he was being dragged away. The lieutenant shrugged half out of his pack and pulled his flashlight from inside, praying the frequent submerging hadn't corroded the batteries. He switched it on. Nothing. He slapped it against his palm and it flickered, so he slapped it some more, and then a white beam burst forth. Shoji trained it on the darkness before him.

Then wished he hadn't.

The narrow beam picked out half a dozen pairs of eyes, reflecting yellow, set wide apart and barely above the water. They were no more than thirty feet away among the trees, and as one, they sank beneath the surface. He turned and panned the light across the opposite flank, seeing a dozen more, some moving closer, most sinking.

He nudged Dai and pointed. “There.”

The gunner let out three short bursts, chopping at the water. The approaching eyes went away.

“Did you hit it?” Shoji yelled. He was a little deaf from being that close to the weapon.

“I can’t tell,” Dai said.

Screaming and gunfire swept up and down the column on both sides, punctuated by long periods of silence. Men were ripped away into the night, their gurgled cries fading out into the trees. In the darkness, it was impossible to tell if the firing hit anything.

Shoji moved up and down both sides of his platoon, speaking with each man, urging them to clean their weapons as best they could, to be careful with their grenades, to hold their ground and stay alert. He saw that a lot of his men were missing.

Another scream from behind them, close enough to hear the accompanying snarl and the sound of roiling water. He saw the shadowy figure of a soldier repeatedly stabbing his bayonet down into the churning swamp, cursing and grunting with each thrust, and then an enormous shape burst from the surface on a different angle and snapped down on him. He wheezed out a bloody mist and was dragged away.

Shoji used his flashlight sparingly, afraid it might draw them in, but unable to resist the urge to know how close they were. Every time he put the beam on the swamp he saw more eyes than before. He also saw that the surface of the water had turned red.

Near the front of the platoon Dai let out a long burst, bullets snapping against mangroves and tearing up the surface, thudding into meatier targets. Another grenade was thrown, this one exploding well out into the trees on the left, the flash destroying Shoji's night vision. He squeezed his eyes tightly shut and rubbed at them, opening them to see absolute blackness sparkling with cracking rifle fire. The line seemed to be holding for the moment.

A pair of figures waded towards him, Nagazawa and an aide.

"Crocodiles," the colonel said tightly.

"Yes!" Shoji said, the word coming out as a shaky laugh. "Crocodiles, not commandos."

The colonel shoved past him. "We're pushing forward. When the platoon ahead of you moves, you follow it. We'll fight as we go." He moved towards the rear.

Shoji had the sudden urge to charge up behind the colonel and push him face first into the bloody water, to beat at him and scream, to punish him for bringing them to this place. Instead he turned and passed the order to his men. Keep moving.

And they did. The column started forward slowly, its trailing elements moving with it like a caterpillar, starting and stopping. The side by side ranks hung close together, eyes and weapons trained outwards as the crocodiles called to each other among the trees. At times their massive shapes were briefly revealed in the moonlight, coasting on the surface for a moment before sinking, and other times only their eyes were visible. Most often they couldn't be seen at all, but they were there, on both sides, and the frequency of their croaking served to let every man in the column know that more and more were arriving.

The attacks continued, though more cautiously, more calculated, as if they were learning about their prey and what their weapons could do. They would ease in slowly, silently, then explode out of the water at close to twenty m.p.h., hitting a victim, clamping down and dragging them under and back. Then came the horrible, violent rolling to dismember the meal, breaking it into palatable sizes. They struck so fast, so unexpectedly and retreated with the same swiftness that few men could get off a shot, and most fired blind.

It went on for hours, the column edging forward through the darkness, the crocodiles striking, picking the men off in savage bursts of crashing water and blood and gunfire. Flashlights cut the night in places with thin, zigzagging beams, catching glimpses of the animals but causing even more confusion. One officer switched on his light and spotlighted the gaping maw and snaggled teeth of a croc a second before it bit his arm off at the shoulder.

Midnight came and went. The cries of terrified and dying men split the night.

And Shoji thought he would go insane.

"Dear God," Fairweather said, "what's happening in there?"

The men on board the patrol boat stood and stared at the swamp, a black silhouette in the moonlight. The occasional pop of a rifle or crackle of a machinegun came from the darkness, and every so often there was a sparkle of light from muzzle flashes or small explosions. Ghostly screams echoed from the darkness and rolled across the water, rising wails that seemed to never end. The screaming had been going on for hours.

Fairweather was reminded of a story his grandfather used to tell at the fireside, a tale of Scotland and the deathly wails of Banshees. As a boy the stories chilled and unsettled him as he imagined what a dreadful, lonely sound that would be. Now on the other side of the world, he no longer had to imagine. They were the most terrible sounds he had ever heard.

"Bastards are killing each other," Sgt. Bremer said, flicking a cigarette butt over the side. "Good."

In the bow, Fairweather shook his head slowly. "No. Something's in there with them."

The sergeant looked at the young man, who simply stared into the darkness.

The screaming and gunfire had of course been reported back to the ships, with all patrol boats confirming they were not in contact with the enemy. Within an hour, orders came back for each boat to move in closer, and for the crew to use their loudhailers to demand the Japanese surrender. Furthermore, there was to be no more firing on Japanese seen at the water's edge, unless fired upon. The new mission was to accept any surrender and capture prisoners.

"What's this bloody nonsense?" Bremer grumbled. "Bloody Navy's gone soft on the Jappers."

Fairweather sighed, relieved that there would be no more killing. Whatever the Japanese were up against in there frightened him, even safe as he was out here on the boat. If he had the chance to show mercy and spare one of those men from whatever it was, he'd be happy to do it.

The five inch guns of the light cruiser fired then, making Fairweather jump and spin, glaring accusingly out at the water where he knew the Phoebe was, while shells whistled overhead. What was this? They just said to offer surrender!

Flares burst over the swamp, floating gently to earth, intense white orbs which lit the mangroves in grays and shadows. More flares were fired, and their sister patrol craft a hundred yards away began calling for surrender on their loudhailer. Sgt. Bremer fired up the engines and began moving the boat in closer to shore, while another marine switched on the craft's bullhorn.

"I guess the Navy figures the Jappers understand English," he grumbled.

13

The Australians called them salties, and took special care around their remote billabongs. Salties there fed on adult kangaroo and wild dogs and anyone foolish enough to get too close to their habitat. Living in an area that stretched from India to Northern Australia, to New Guinea and across the islands of the Pacific Rim, the saltwater crocodile was the largest reptile on earth, a prehistoric species which had adapted, survived and thrived for 200 million years.

Males averaged sixteen feet in length and could weigh up to a ton. For such a large animal, it was swift in the water and even faster on land for short distances, capable of running down prey and crushing it in powerful jaws. They were apex predators, fearless killers which could travel across open ocean – some made an annual migration back and forth between New Zealand and

Southeast Asia – and fed on sharks when the opportunity presented itself. Salties were aggressive and territorial, masters of ambush who were drawn by the splashing of prey, sound, and the scent of blood.

Shoji Kichida neither knew nor cared about any of this. He was up to his chest in the water, one arm hooked around a shrieking young soldier, trying to keep him from being pulled away. A crocodile had one of the boy's legs clamped in its jaws, and was yanking him backwards, away from the column. Around them, every man was engaged as the crocs came at them on both sides, some firing, some using bayonets or rifle butts, all of them yelling.

The boy was shrieking in his ear as Shoji fought to hold onto him, aiming his pistol at the dark shape and squeezing off two rounds before the slide locked back on an empty magazine. The muzzle flash showed him a ridged, scarred head two feet wide. He couldn't have missed at this range, but the creature didn't seem to notice. It gave a sharp tug, and the leg came away at the knee.

The boy howled, and sagged back against the lieutenant.

Another croc rushed in next to them, a fast-moving black wall close enough that one of its paddling claws tore a gouge in Shoji's shoulder. It snapped onto another soldier and bore him down.

Shoji struggled to get his feet under him, to pull the boy back to the line. The croc let out a roar, the leg partially down its throat, then lunged forward and sank its jaws into the boy's midsection, shaking its head like a dog with a rag, tearing him from Shoji's grip. Blood burst from the boy's mouth and Shoji heard bones snap as the creature gave him another shake, retreated a dozen yards before beginning its roll.

The lieutenant managed to stand and fumbled for another clip for his pistol. The pouch was empty.

Flares burst overhead, turning the swamp into a swinging landscape of light and dark. Eyes were revealed, glimmering yellow on the surface, dozens of pairs moving in rapidly, frenzied over the smells and sounds. A machinegun rattled behind him, and a grenade went off. Shoji tore off his pack, dug the three grenades out from within and one by one, slammed the arming pins into the trunk of a mangrove. Then he hurled them into the trees towards the eyes.

Three explosions went off in succession, adding bursts of fire to the white glare from overhead. He saw several crocodiles heave upwards with the blast and roll over.

"Die!" he screamed. "Die! Die!"

All around him men were fighting for their lives, black and white shadows moving in slow motion, trying desperately to keep away from monsters three times their size and twenty times their weight. Just to their rear, one of the regiment's remaining flamethrowers went into action, its operator triggering thirty yard belches of a flaming gasoline and tar mixture. He swept it across the surface of the water immediately in front of him, then further back into the trees. Now the water was burning, as were some of the mangroves. In seconds the flaming shapes of tarantulas and scorpions were dropping from the canopy.

The soldier raised his muzzle and waded to the opposite side, sweeping that flank in the same manner. There were hoarse cheers as the men saw crocodiles set afire, only to watch them immediately submerge. It took less than two minutes for the twelve liter tanks to run dry, and then the soldier simply shed his fifty-seven pound burden and let it fall into the water.

Dai appeared beside Shoji and began firing short, controlled bursts, his face grim and set in the light from the flares. Rounds chopped up the trees and water, and Shoji saw his weapon finding its mark among their attackers, big dark bodies sinking beneath the surface, some rolling to float belly up. The attacks abruptly ceased.

Dai stopped firing, and Shoji reached for the man's pack. "I'll reload you."

The gunner shook his head. "That was my last belt." He looked at his officer. "It's just useless weight now." He started to unsling the machinegun.

"No!" Shoji put his hands on the hot weapon. "We'll redistribute ammo from the other gunners."

“We’ve been doing that already,” he said, pulling the weapon away and taking the sling off his shoulders. “Everyone’s out.” He tossed the machinegun into the water, where it hissed for an instant before sinking.

Shoji stared out into the swamp, lit now in the hellish glow of fuel patches burning on the water, and mangrove trees with tendrils of fire clinging to their damp trunks. The stink of burnt tar competed with the hot, coppery tang of blood. He remembered reading Dante at university, and decided the man must have visited Ramree.

You are truly in hell, Shoji’s unpleasant voice whispered, as fire danced in his eyes, mesmerizing. *You have crossed some threshold, and now pass through the Underworld. The demons are among us, feasting at their leisure. You will never leave this place.*

This time Shoji knew the voice was right.

Soon Colonel Nagazawa’s ragged voice bellowed for the regiment to reform and get moving. As they came together and started forward, Cpl. Yoichi reported that the platoon was down to nine men. Shoji grunted in acknowledgement but barely heard him, wading forward into the darkening swamp as the last flare sputtered overhead, drawing his family sword, the only weapon he had left.

14

The British loudspeakers called from beyond the trees throughout the night, hollow voices speaking in a language none of them understood. Shoji assumed they were probably offers for surrender, and the naval guns kept firing flares presumably to facilitate that surrender, but the colonel insisted that their enemies were merely taunting the embattled regiment. It made no difference either way. Even if the colonel would permit it – and he still clung to his determination to deliver his force to Burma – anyone wanting to surrender would have to leave the dubious safety of the column and cross the mangroves to get to the sea, through the darkness, past the jaws of waiting killers.

They were no longer in waist deep water. It had quickly gone to their knees, then their shins, then to a several inch layer of brine before disappearing completely, leaving mud beneath their feet. The tide hadn't gone out. The terrain was rising, and now the thin column was treading through the mangroves in an area which rarely saw water, among hummocks of dry dirt and grasses. By then the remaining men were too weary to notice or care.

Cpl. Yoichi had died around two a.m. Shoji hadn't witnessed it, but a private reported seeing the man bitten nearly in half by a monster which erupted from the water without warning, struck, and carried the corporal back under.

Cpl. Dai perished an hour later, and Shoji had seen that death, the big man stabbing furiously with a bayonet in one hand even as his killer was ripping off his other arm. Men hit the crocodile with rifle butts and helmets – no one had any ammunition left by that point – but the croc took him anyway.

Neither man lived long enough to feel dry land. Theirs weren't the only deaths.

It was now past four. Shoji's dysentery wracked him with regular cramps, and he was running a high fever. It made thinking difficult, and every once in a while he saw Satcheko standing among the mangroves. Sometimes she wore a white kimono and beckoned to him with open arms. Other times she was charred and skeletal, one eye blazing with unspoken accusations. Occasionally he heard her calling his name, but he did not go to her.

The 121st Imperial Infantry Regiment ceased to exist in the early hours of February 21st, 1945. They had succeeded in traveling nearly nine miles of the twelve mile stretch to the Burmese mainland.

It was the instinctive behavior of female crocodiles to claw out nests in dry earth and then line and covered them with grass before laying their eggs and settling in to stand watch. Nesting made them especially territorial. The mating season itself made the bulls, already aggressive by their nature, even more dangerous. The mating season for saltwater crocodiles ran from November to March.

The mangroves of Ramree Island had been a nesting ground for thousands of years. At any given time the area boasted a salty population in excess of a thousand adults. At five a.m. on that morning, as the sky was turning a coral pink overhead, Colonel Kanichi Nagazawa led the one-hundred sixteen survivors of his regiment straight into the largest crocodile nest in Southern Asia.

Shoji was thirty feet away when he saw the colonel, who had been walking point for hours, pause on a grassy hummock up ahead and turn to face his men. An enormous black and gray male exploded out of the grasses behind him, snapped down on both his legs at the knees, and threw him onto his face. An instant later a pair of females ran in from both sides, one seizing an arm and a shoulder, the other biting down on his head. He was torn apart in seconds.

Crocodiles roared all around them, racing in swiftly and hitting the column from every angle, hurling bodies to the ground, shaking them apart, dragging screaming men away into the grassy hummocks. A smaller female charged Shoji, and he let out a cry just as it was about to bite and drove his sword down through the top of its head, piercing its brain and bringing the creature to a sliding halt. He jerked the blade free and swung at another, severing one of its forelegs. Undaunted, it twisted to snap at him but stumbled, off balance, and Shoji thrust the sword deep through one of its eyes, killing it instantly.

"Shoji!"

The lieutenant whirled to see Tatsuya dangling from the jaws of a huge bull, bitten nearly in two, his intestines trailing out behind him as the croc retreated into the grasses with its prize. Blood spilled from his friend's mouth as he gurgled, *"Kill me!"*

Shoji charged after the beast, sword raised, and then saw it give a violent shake. Tatsuya's torso came apart.

"No!" Shoji screamed, watching the creature tilt back its head and choke down his friend's lower half with a grunt. The ground was covered in giant, moving shapes and fallen men, fresh blood sharp in the air, nearly overpowered by a sour, reptilian musk, screams and inhuman roaring filling his head. He saw soldiers scattering and running into the trees, and then he was running too.

He moved as fast as he could, his water-deprived muscles quivering and threatening to seize up, lurching through the mangroves, still clinging to his sword. His bowels were twisting, and the fever made his vision swim, causing him to collide with trees and then rebound off to stagger on. There was movement on the ground, long dark shapes in the early light croaking and opening jaws, and he wove around them, summoning fear-fueled reserves of strength, leaping over one crocodile which twisted and snapped, nearly catching his leg.

He ran towards the sounds of the loudspeakers.

Huge shapes rustled through the underbrush all around him, and he caught sight of a handful of men running through the mangroves, heading in the same direction he was. Several fell and didn't get up, and for a few seconds a shrieking boy of sixteen was running beside him, arms and legs pumping. There was a snarl and a blur of movement from the right, and then the boy was gone, making wet, gasping noises behind him.

Shoji splashed through shallow pools of water, swept through tangles of leaves swarming with biting ants, stumbled through a black cloud of mosquitoes which blinded him and choked his mouth and nose. Still he ran.

He heard crashing behind him, something big bumping and scraping against mangrove trunks, heard the throaty grunt as it pursued him. Shoji began dodging left and right, around trees, not giving it a direct line of attack, denying it the speed it was capable of as it tried to follow him, but despite his efforts it remained close. He didn't dare look back.

Suddenly the sea was before him, dazzling and blue, a salty breeze rushing over his body. He lurched into water which surged against his thighs, squinting at the sudden openness and light. Thirty yards offshore sat a gray patrol boat with a Union Jack at the stern, and beyond, out on the deeper, tranquil blue, a pair of warships rode at anchor, powerful and majestic in the pink light.

All illusions of duty and tigers and Bushido burned away like fog in the morning sun as he realized he would make it. He would give himself to the enemy, ride out the war as a POW, and when the Allies won – as they surely would – he would be returned to his beloved Satcheko. They would marry and go for long walks in the cold snowfall, and he would forget all about this place.

Shoji waded in to his hips and started yelling at the figures on the patrol boat.

Men were coming out of the trees at the same time, spread out across the shore of the swamp, perhaps two dozen in all. They immediately headed into the water. Fairweather saw his sister boat motoring in towards some of these men, and felt the deck of his own boat shudder as Sgt. Bremer brought them in as close as he dared.

"That one," the sergeant yelled, pointing. "He's got officer's insignia on his shoulders."

Fairweather looked. The sergeant was pointing at the man closest to their boat, pushing forward into the water and looking over his shoulder.

"Over the side, Fairweather," Bremer called. "Go get him."

The private slung his sub machinegun across his chest and did as ordered, slipping over and into waist-deep, warm water. He gripped his weapon and started through the shallows. He had never seen a Japanese up close, and half expected him to have horns and a tail. But this was just a man, bone thin and unshaven, his torn and bloody uniform hanging on him like a loose sack. The Japanese was struggling towards him through the water, still looking back.

Shoji saw it emerge from the trees, a monstrosity close to twenty feet long with a three foot wide head. Snaggled, yellow teeth protruded from its upper and lower jaws. The creature slid languidly into the water behind him, its powerful tail propelling it forward. Shoji saw the boy moving towards him, young and nervous with his weapon half raised. He hadn't seen it. He raised his arms and began waving. "Crocodile! Go back! Go back!"

Oh, God, he's got a sword! Fairweather looked at the wild-eyed man coming at him, waving the long blade, screaming in Japanese. *It's one of those insane*

Kamikazes! The private jerked his weapon up and pointed it at the shouting man.

"Drop the sword! Stand where you are! Drop the sword!"

Shoji didn't know what the boy was saying, only that he hadn't seen it yet. "Get back! Get back in the boat!" He raised his sword over his head and took it in both hands, shaking it, hoping to scare him back to safety.

The Jap was crazy, half dead but still ready to kill one more Brit. Fairweather's finger tensed on the trigger. "Stand where you are or I'll shoot!" Then he saw it, the dark mass rushing through the water behind the Japanese, and he suddenly understood.

A rifle cracked close behind him, and Fairweather felt more than heard the buzz of the bullet overhead. The Japanese went down, crashing backwards into the surf, into the path of the monster.

"Goddamnit, Fairweather," yelled Bremer, holding the rifle. "Were you going to just wait until that fucking nip chopped your head off?"

Fairweather didn't hear him. He was scrambling back to the boat, thrashing through the water and screaming for his crewmates to pull him up, pull him up right bloody now!

Shoji felt the bullet hit him in the chest and blow the wind out of him, knock him over to land on his back, felt the warm surf wash over him. It didn't hurt, and he felt himself going to sleep. Coral skies shaded with hints of pale blue soared overhead, pink tinged clouds marching gracefully along. He barely felt the jaws close on him. Sleep was coming on quickly and he sensed he was moving, cruising backwards through the water, a tight, warm pressure in his chest, almost comforting. Perhaps he would dream of Satcheko. Perhaps when he awoke she would be there, her beautiful face smiling above him.

The sword slipped from his grasp and sank into the shallows.

The men on the patrol boat were too busy hauling the new kid back on board to see the long, dark shape emerge from the water with something sagging in its jaws, turning and moving into the mangroves.

Also by John L. Campbell

Red Circus: A Dark Collection

And watch for

IN THE FALLING LIGHT

Macabre Tales

Made in the USA
Charleston, SC
14 August 2014